Alessandra
in Love

Alessandra in Love

Robert Kaplow

J. B. LIPPINCOTT   NEW YORK

Alessandra in Love is a work of fiction. All names, characters, and events are fictional, and any resemblance to real persons or actual events is unintentional.

I would like to give special thanks to Sally Doherty for her help with this book.

R.K.

Grateful acknowledgement is made for permission to reprint an exerpt from "Joy to the World." Words and music by Hoyt Axton. Copyright © 1971 by Lady Jane Music. All rights reserved. Reprinted by permission.

Library of Congress Cataloging-in-Publication Data
Kaplow, Robert.
  Alessandra in love / Robert Kaplow.
    p.   cm.
  Summary: Driven by her romantic dreams, sixteen-year-old Alessandra reveals
through the pages of her journal how she is mesmerized by the self-centered
musician Wyn, "in spite of everything."
  ISBN 0-397-32281-X : $ ISBN 0-397-32282-8 (lib. bdg.) : $
  [1. Diaries.]   I. Title.
PZ7.K1176A1 1989   88-23141
[Fic]—dc19   CIP
                                                          AC

to my sister Terry

Alessandra
in Love

One

I can't seem to get Wyn Reed off my mind. I've spent the last half hour blasting music through the house, dancing by myself in the living room. I think if anybody saw me, they'd have me arrested. I'm a pretty wild dancer when no one's around.

Let me describe Wyn. First, of course, he's got the *face*. I don't know what it is, but there's a certain kind of face that consistently throws me off-balance. The face isn't classically handsome; I doubt many people would even stop to look twice at it—it's too elusive, too cold—but somehow it attracts me.

And this is *not* just another suicidal romantic obsession. I mean, I've had enough of those this week.

This guy is a serious candidate for Mr. Adequate. When he walked into orchestra the other day, I took one look and my heart stood up and sang the Hallelujah Chorus. He had just moved here from Millburn, and he's a senior. Perlmacher introduced him to the orchestra. "Ladies and gentlemen, I'd like you to meet Wyn Reed." And there was this tall kid with the palest skin I had ever seen—and these dark, dark eyes. He wore a black short-sleeved shirt and tan trousers. He stood with his cello case under the stage lights looking embarrassed and smiling uncomfortably. But there was something amused and confident in those eyes—something suggesting that all the modesty was an artfully conceived performance, that he *knew* how good he was, that he knew he was better than any string player on that stage.

It was a look of self-assurance I'd seen before. Last year the *face* had belonged to Bayard Lees. I was looking at Bayard's photograph in the yearbook the other day, and I was somewhat ashamed to notice that much of his magic still persisted. But I was only a callow tenth grader then. There he was—Bayard Lees, one of those kids who seemed to have popularity and ease born into them. He sang in a rock band called Techno-Lust. He looked like Jim Morrison if Jim Morrison were fifteen and had bad teeth. Wild brown hair, torn shirt, suede boots with cowboy fringe. He carried a copy of *No One Here Gets Out Alive* next to his Latin book. Like every other girl in the school, I was in love with him, or at least I thought I was.

So I did what every fifteen-year-old does in that kind of situation. I stole his English folder. I figured that if I read his essays, I'd at least learn something about him. One day after school, when the custodian had left the teachers' rooms unlocked to clean them, I lifted his folder from the filing cabinet. This is not a confession that inspires me with much pride. I swear I was sweating, I was so sure I'd get caught.

That night I closed my door, sat up in bed, and carefully read his paragraphs on "The Secret Life of Walter Mitty" and "The Most Dangerous Game." I studied his vocabulary quizzes and his punctuation exercises. I labored over his book report on *Childhood's End.*

The only thing I learned was that he couldn't spell the word "definitely." He also had a lot of trouble with "receive." Hours of my life I had spent watching this guy, reading the irony of his brown eyes, listening to every word he said in class as if it were the key to his heart. I had spent half a year investing him with a poet's magic . . . and there was nothing there.

But did the truth stop me? Certainly not.

One night, under the influence of a passionate loneliness, I sent him a letter. It was anonymous, of course. My father has reams of this creamy-gray construction paper, and I neatly typed in the middle of one sheet: *You have a beautiful soul, Bayard.* I bicycled to the next town to mail it. It was raining, and the more soaked I got, the more I felt I was suffering a deserved punishment for my own reckless stupidity. I looked at the letter one last time. I placed it in the drawer of the mailbox and let it close. There was no stopping it now. "What are you doing, Alessandra?" I said out loud. "What ridiculous thing are you doing now?" Looking back a year later, I write these things with a certain cynicism, but at the time there was nothing cynical or humorous about it. I see myself then as a glum little ghost. I remember waking up in the morning, looking in the mirror, and being surprised that I looked like a normal human being.

Well, about a month after mailing him the letter, we were all at the tenth-grade picnic at Sandy Hook. I'd spent the day walking the shore with my best friend, Melissa, a bright-red towel draped around me to hide the fact that I'm a little overweight. For a while I watched Bayard play tennis with our history teacher. I liked the way he crouched in concentration before each serve. I liked the sharp *pock* of the ball hitting his racket.

Melissa and I sat giggling on the bench like true addled-escents.

"Alessandra," Bayard called to me, "do you want to play?"

I laughed. "I don't know how." I pulled the towel closer around me. Melissa was dying.

"I'll teach you."

"No, no. I'd rather watch."

He shrugged. "Does your friend want to play?"

Melissa turned scarlet and exploded in laughter. She left eventually, but I stayed and sort of shared in the energy and exhaustion of their game. They took a break and stood near me, drinking sodas and mopping their brows.

I sat reading in my one-piece leopard-spotted bathing suit.

"Alessandra," said Mr. Aviano, "that report of yours on Charles Beard was one of the most brilliant student essays I've ever read."

I looked up and smiled.

Bayard—his Jim Morrison hair all wild with sweat —was suddenly interested. "Can I read it?" he asked. "If Aviano says it's brilliant, then it must be something."

"Alessandra is one of the best writers in the school."

"You're embarrassing me."

Mr. Aviano laughed. "And everything she turns in is on this weird gray construction paper. I can tell it's her work before I even look at the heading."

Bayard's gentle glance was like a bullet into my heart. He was fast. He'd made the connection in an instant. I looked down. *You have a beautiful soul, Bayard.*

"As soon as I get an essay on gray paper, I know it's Alessandra's. I usually put it on the bottom of the pile just to give myself something to look forward to."

Bayard was kind enough never to mention it.

All right, bring up the violins. Long shot: Alessandra walking barefoot on the sand, crying behind her oversized glasses.

Why do I have to relive every painful episode in my life? The most exhausting part is that I waste my time imagining other ways it might have turned out. I spend half my life replaying conversations in my head and fixing up the dialogue so it comes out right.

Now I hear the front door opening, the hall door slamming, and the television blare.

"Alessandra, anybody call?" asks my mother.

"No."

I wait for them to find something to criticize me about—the bathroom isn't neat enough; the kitchen has a crumb in the sink.

I wish my parents would go on vacation for a while.

If it weren't near midnight, I'd take another shower. It's the only time I feel at ease. I probably waste more water than anyone on the East Coast. I love the perfume of shampoo, the rush of steam, and my radio blaring out the Bards of Passion. *"Detoxify your heart!"* sings Throb, and I sing along.

Melissa bought me a huge ceiling poster of Throb for my birthday. He's wearing a torn T-shirt and mirror sunglasses. He looks as if he needs a shave.

Ode to Throb
by Alessandra F. Hogarth
Throb, Throb, Throb, Throb,
Throb, Throb, Throb, Throb,
Throb, Throb, Throb, Throb,
Take off all your clothes.

I always knew I had a flair for lyric poetry.

Well, it's now past midnight, and all I've got is sixty pages of collateral reading to finish for history, a chemistry lab to copy over, and an essay on nihilism in *Lord of the Flies* to write for English. Hey, another night with two hours of sleep, another morning without breakfast, and A.F.H. is ready to face the world!

I keep thinking about the various guys I've been hung up on. *Why?* I mean, who wants to write any more letters on gray paper? Who wants to watch the clock turn to four in the morning and you haven't slept one minute because you've been thinking about some idiot who doesn't even care that you exist? Isn't there a time in your life when you stop chasing people? Stop begging them to love you?

Two

I think I am truly in love!

I'm writing now in French class, where my well-behaved friend Melissa K. Silverman is sitting next to me, trying not to burst out laughing. Poor Monsieur Bauer has his fly wide open. The rest of the class is pretty cool about this, but Ms. Silverman is so immature she's about to choke with laughter. I do believe she's turning pink. Her complexion just about matches the frames of her glasses. Poor Monsieur Bauer has pulled down a map and is passionately lecturing us on the great Parisian sewer system. This is somewhat amusing, considering.

Melissa is wearing her madras peasant dress and

her sixteen silver bangle bracelets. She was clearly born twenty years too late. She walks around barefoot. She draws peace signs on her notebook and actually uses the word "groovy" in conversation. Any girl who has smiling-face stickers on her notebook—what can you say? But at least she likes the Bards of Passion. She does have *some* taste.

We've decided to go to the June-in-January beachparty dance. I will wear the most outrageous bathing suit I can find; I'll probably get thrown out.

I've known Wyn for about a week now. The only class we share is orchestra. I swear my heart beats faster as each day draws near seventh period. My best days are "B" and "E" days, when we get a long seventh. I can relax enough to study him. It's a little annoying that from where I sit, my view of him is partially obstructed by the violas. But visible always are his miraculous, long, pale hands. I like the way his fingers arch in a sweet vibrato.

He plays beautifully. I bend my neck to try to glimpse his face, those astonishing dark eyes, the startling lock of gray hair. He's always dressed in browns and blacks—always short-sleeved shirts.

His cello case leans against some scenery behind where I sit. I've made a careful study of it. It's got a sticker printed with a G clef and the words "New

Jersey Youth Symphony." It's got another sticker that says "This cello belongs to:"—and handwritten beneath it in black ballpoint is "Wyn Reed" with his old Millburn address and phone number. There's a blue airline baggage check attached to the handle.

He drives a pale-blue Volkswagen van. It's got a bunch of college parking stickers on the side window; I haven't gotten close enough yet to read what colleges they are.

He's actually quite friendly to me. I introduced myself the other day as another student who had moved in from out of town. He smiled.

I kept thinking, as I talked to him, that he looked like Boo Radley in *To Kill a Mockingbird*—the same impression that he hadn't seen daylight in a long while, his dark eyes in shocking contrast to the paleness of his face.

He asked me about the June-in-January dance after orchestra.

"If you come in a bathing suit it's only a dollar," I said.

"That ought to be funny. All these people in bathing suits walking through the snow."

"You should go, Wyn."

"Maybe I will."

Oh, I was *dying* to ask him. But of course I didn't.

13

I repeated every detail to Melissa back in my bedroom.

"I would have asked."

"Me*lee*ssa."

She laughed. "So when are you going to call him?"

"Call him? Why are you always suggesting these ridiculous things?"

"It's not ridiculous."

"Then why don't *you* ever do these things you think of? 'Come on, Alessandra, let's go to New York and see a pornographic movie.' Great idea, right? As long as I buy the tickets."

"I don't look eighteen! Well, is he at least going to be there tonight, Alessandra?"

"Do you think I care? Do you think I'm going to tear myself to pieces over some guy? No way."

"I like your attitude."

"Just call me Miss Cool."

Suddenly Melissa held her hand to her head and cried out, "I'm a *jerrrrrrrk!*"

I answered back in a scream: "I'm *faaaaaaat!*"

This was an old game of ours we used to play when we stayed home every Friday night.

"I'm a *jerrrrrrrk!*" she cried out again.

"I'm *faaaaaaat!*"

"Yes, but you can always lose weight, and I'm still a *jerrrrrrk!*"

The walk to school was exhilarating. The wind was deliciously cold, and we wore only topcoats over our bathing suits. From a distance the school looked like a supermarket at the North Pole—white fluorescent lights burning in a field of snow. There was music pounding. You could hear it from the sidewalk. Inside, crepe-paper streamers flew from the lights. Nearly half the people wore bathing suits, sandals, or shorts—all blindingly colorful—spitting right in the face of January, and I couldn't have been happier. Melissa and I stood with the other girls for a while, but when they played the Bards of Passion it was as if someone had yanked a string inside me. I shrieked, leaped up, and danced with Melissa. I love to dance. And I don't mind dancing with another girl—it's a private thing anyway.

We danced barefoot for about an hour. I was sweating and out of breath, the blood pumping hard in my head. Then we sat by the windows and watched the other dancers. We drew our initials in the condensation on the glass. The crowd was large, and there was a hot, wild energy in the air. I looked at the couples sailing in the dark, embracing, flying with the music. Then the lights were dimmed, and they played some slow, romantic song. To hear it and watch the couples in each other's arms made me feel kind of lonely. It really could have been summer for a moment. The room was warm; the music was slow. I watched the guys dancing in nothing but cutoffs. I closed my eyes. If I could just change the world, transfigure it with my imagination, it could be me dancing; it could be me at ease with myself.

Melissa tapped me on the shoulder. She nodded toward the crowd. "Your friend Wyn."

There was my pale cellist, still dressed in his black short-sleeved shirt and tan trousers. He was dancing without much interest and without much grace. His partner was a tall, self-assured-looking girl. She had wonderful shoulders and curly brown hair. She wore white shorts, a wildly colorful shirt, sandals, and sunglasses with strings.

"Who is she?"

"I don't know."

"Is she a senior?"

I watched them for a few minutes. Then the disc jockey played another slow dance record. I groaned. Wyn and his girlfriend were gone in the dark mass of music and bodies.

There was a time when I would have stayed and watched them the rest of the evening. I might even have followed them home. But I was trying to leave that stuff behind me.

We walked back to Melissa's house singing every Bards of Passion song we knew, alternating verses and singing together on the choruses. We danced around the traffic lights and made comments about all the people we could see in their houses.

"Look—Suzy Homemaker and Hubby."

"He teaches gym."

"Met him at the beach. Married him because of his body. Now she realizes he's a superficial jerk who likes to polish his car and barbecue on the gas grill." I pointed to an upstairs light across the street. "Joe Motorhead entertains his girlfriend while his parents are out taking their course on aerobic dancing."

I grabbed some snow off a bush and tried to put it down Melissa's back. She screamed and threw snow in my hair. The iciness was pleasant. I thought, Look around you, Alessandra. There are funny things to see. Beauty to breathe. Lay off romance for a while. You've seen too many movies. Stop trying to force everything to happen. When it happens, it happens.

Detoxify your heart, Alessandra.

Three

Alert the media. I had my first real date with Wyn tonight—the first real date in my life!

We had been walking out of orchestra together for a while. He's an average-built guy, but he's got these great arms. I suppose that comes from playing the cello. And he's left-handed! All left-handed people are cool. I think it's because they use the right side of the brain—the freaky side.

We kind of hit it off because we're always laughing about how bad the orchestra sounds. I watch him as the strings enter with their unbelievably dissonant blast—"the wall of pain," he calls it. He contorts his face with comic anguish while the strings screech around him like a thousand cats howling for their guts back. Wyn says that not only is Tchaikovsky turning over in his grave, he's setting land-speed records.

Then the strings grow quiet, and it's time for the woodwinds to hammer their nail into the coffin. Looking over my flute, I see Wyn giving me a mock-rhapsodic smile as all around the reeds start squeaking and wailing and spitting. It's so bad it makes your eyes water.

But at least all this awfulness had given us something to talk about. There were times when I'd be standing next to him along the back curtains, just killing time on the five-minute break, and I couldn't believe he was actually talking to me. I didn't know what I was saying; it felt as if there were a blast furnace in my chest.

The most revealing moment until our date tonight was when I unexpectedly came upon him during lunch. It was a "C" day, when I don't see Melissa, and I wandered out on the loading dock to get away from all the noise in the cafeteria. I like the loading dock. I can sit on a plastic milk box, watch the trees, and hide for a little while.

This time I opened the door, and there was Wyn leaning against the brick wall. It was raining heavily.

"Hey," I said.

He seemed pleased to see me. "Hey."

"You look like you're posing for an album cover," I said.

He smiled. "The guy from Deutsche Grammophon is supposed to get here any minute."

"Do you mind if I sit here for a while? I was looking for a quiet place to finish my yogurt." I sat on a milk box.

"I always see you carrying that little book," he said. "Is it a diary?"

"It's my journal. I like to write."

"I wish I did. I got a C plus last marking period in English; Sullivan said it was a grade of complete mercy." He gave me a wonderfully goofy grin. "On Fridays I bring my cello to class and play Beatles songs for him. Can you believe it? I'm selling out for a passing grade. You've never lived till you've heard my solo rendition of 'Penny Lane.' It sounds like the 'Penny Lane Minuet.'" He laughed. "My corruption knows no bounds."

He glanced at the dark sky.

"It's really coming down," I said.

"And I have to drive into New York this afternoon. Ugh. On a Friday in the rain. What a nightmare."

"Can't you get out of it?"

"I have a lesson."

I nodded and ate another spoonful of yogurt.

"I like that necklace, Alexandra."

"Ale*ssan*dra. It's interlocking plastic fruit. You can rearrange it any way you like. Sometimes I put all the bananas together. Other times I alternate colors."

"Very stylish."

"All the writers are wearing them," I said. "How long have you been studying the cello?"

He placed his fingertips together. He was tapping his foot to a melody in his head. "Since sixth grade."

A car suddenly screeched into the parking lot, and two kids jumped out holding bags from a fast-food restaurant.

"Escape from Cell Block Eight," said Wyn, watching them.

"One's father is the chief of police," I said. "The other's father is the superintendent of schools."

He laughed. "That figures. I've always heard the worst kids in school are the sons of teachers and the sons of cops."

"Also the sons of child psychologists."

"In Millburn last year, on the first day it snowed,

this real maniac—who was a teacher's kid—went out on the lawn and made a six-foot sculpture of a male sexual organ in the snow."

"He'll probably grow up and teach A.P. Biology."

"What I really remember about that snow was this awful ride to New York. I had just gotten my license then, and you know you're not even supposed to drive in New York till you're eighteen. There I was in this blizzard. Traffic at a standstill. And I'm sitting in the Holland Tunnel for forty minutes. Just sitting in the tunnel, not moving."

"I would have started screaming."

"It was maybe the worst day in my life. I had to audition for Juilliard precollege that afternoon. I'm sitting in the tunnel—*illegally*. I'm staring at my watch, certain that I'm never going to make it, that somebody's going to check my license. I see my whole life falling to pieces in the middle of the Holland Tunnel. I've just had this huge argument with my girlfriend. Now I'm going to be late for the audition. My van is overheating. It's snowing. And I'm stuck in the tunnel. I'm thinking: Just let me die here. Just let me die quietly here on the front seat."

"Did you finally make it in?"

He nodded. "I felt like I'd lost about five years of

my life." He shook his head. "Haven't you ever wished you were like those two clowns just now? No responsibilities, just running out to Burger King? Sometimes that seems like a very appealing life."

"The problem is that they're probably jealous of your life. And your talent."

"A girl I know says that whenever something good happens in your life—like getting into Juilliard—it comes walking hand in hand with something equally bad."

"This girl must be a blast at parties," I said.

"She also says, 'Tough times go on and on. But tough people eventually drop dead.'"

"She *does* sound fun. Let me write that one down."

He smiled. "Do you ever go anywhere without that notebook?"

"I like to write down funny things that happen to me."

"Do you let other people read it?"

"Only my analyst."

"Are you going to write down this conversation?"

"Never," I said.

He looked at his watch and stood up to leave. "Got to talk to Perlmacher."

I nodded to him.

"Take care, Alexandra," he said. "Give my best to your analyst." He walked back into the school.

"Ale*ssan*dra," I said.

Need I add that Melissa had been following this developing friendship with an attitude that wavered somewhere between maternal concern and psychotic jealousy.

"Aren't you going to see him after school someday?" she asked as we walked home through the drifts of snow.

"He doesn't have the time. He's always running to New York. He's got lessons and recitals."

"And how about the girl he was dancing with? Who was she, his cello teacher?"

"You're so immature, Melissa."

"*I'm* immature? I'm not the one wearing pink pants and green sneakers."

"They're not green; they're aqua."

"They go so well with your Girl Scout scarf."

"Are we talking about *clothes* now, Melissa? Has our conversation sunk that low?"

"All I want, Alessandra, are some details about the guy, that's all."

"Mel*ee*ssa—"

"It's normal, healthy curiosity."

"You, *healthy*? That's a laugh," I said. "You're the only person I know who gets excited by the shape of Florida."

"You're the one who pointed it out!"

"Yes, but I was only joking. You went out and bought an atlas."

We dodged a snowball fight being waged across opposite sides of the street.

"So you're serious about him, huh?" said Melissa.

"It's extremely casual, I told you. I don't expect the baby for another few months."

"Thank God you waited."

"The problem, Mel, is that you take a little casual friendship and you blow it up into the romance of the century. Can't we be adults about this?"

"Adults? Absolutely. You want to stop in town? I hear Throb's on the cover of the new *Teen Beat.*"

"Bitchin'."

"Groovy."

Let me get back to the date. Today Wyn was carrying his cello case down the hall, and I struck up a conversation. I walked out to his van with him.

"Another boring Friday," I said.

"Another boring week." He slid his cello into the back of the van.

"Were things any better in Millburn?"

"Well, the orchestra was better. I tell you, when the strings come in on that Schubert piece, I hear huge plates of glass breaking somewhere."

"How much is this thing worth?" I said, helping him lock the cello in place.

"About seven thousand in the case. About sixty-five hundred out of the case. About thirty dollars if I'm playing. The best thing I play is the theme from *Jaws.*"

"That's why you're studying at Juilliard."

"Precollege. Not a colossal achievement."

"Better than most people."

"We'll see if they give me any money."

"For next year, you mean?"

"I'm up for the David Blair Toub scholarship. It's a lot of money. If I could get that, I could relax."

"You're certainly good enough."

He shrugged. "Everybody in precollege is good."

His eyes darted restlessly around the parking lot. The winter sun accentuated his pale skin and brought out the red in his hair.

"Well, I wish you luck," I said.

He smiled. "Thank you, Alessandra. You'll notice I said it right this time."

"Yes. Anyone who calls me 'Alexandra' more than twice is permanently denied my friendship."

26

"I'll be very careful."

"Why do you wear short-sleeved shirts in winter? Aren't you cold?" I asked.

"I'm fine."

He was wearing one of his black shirts. His folded arms shone in the hard sunlight. I was standing there in the parking lot acting cool as could be, and my legs were shaking. I cleaned my glasses to steady myself.

"So what colleges are you applying to?" he asked. He drummed his fingers nervously on the window of his van.

"I could lie," I said. "Thousands would. But I'm only a junior."

"Oh, right."

"Some guy in the Short Hills mall the other day asked me what college I was going to."

"What did you say?"

"I said I was a freshman at B.U."

He laughed. "I tell you, Alessandra, you're more intelligent and certainly a lot funnier than most of the seniors around here."

"Thank you," I said. "I've got to ask you this. Is that really gray hair?"

He touched the ash-blond streak on his forehead. "It happened about a year ago. I think it came from nerves."

"What are you so nervous about?"

"Music mostly."

The bell rang. We headed back inside. I was happy to walk next to him. I wanted to ask more about his music, but I felt it was getting too personal. Still, I wanted to keep the conversation going.

"And so another seventh period draws to a close," I said.

Inside the school, you could hear the shouting of kids running to beat the lunch lines.

"And so Wyn and Alessandra walk back to class," he said, "wondering what's on each other's minds."

I looked at him.

We were heading toward the loading-dock stairs.

He took a deep breath. "So what are you doing tonight?"

All around people were yelling, throwing their books. Cans of soda were coming out of the lockers. You could feel the madness of a Friday afternoon. Far down the hall I could see Melissa heading my way. I thought: Stay away for one minute, Melissa.

"What would you want to do?" I asked.

As we walked, he ran a finger along a groove in the tiled wall. "Well, we could sit on your porch, and I could play the theme from *Jaws* on my cello."

28

"We haven't got a porch."

"We could go to the movies," he said. "Your standard cliché date."

"A *date*? Is that what this is?"

"You tell me."

"Do we go to a diner afterward and have carrot cake—like they do in the movies?"

"If you insist."

"Then do you walk me to my door, where we shake hands, and you say, 'So am I going to see you again, Alessandra?' "

He laughed. "You've seen more movies than I have."

"We have cable."

The late bell rang.

"Oh, I don't know what to do," I said. And I thought: Why am I playing hard to get like this? But I couldn't stop. "There's no movie I'm dying to see."

"We could do the diner. There's one on North Avenue, right? I don't know if they serve carrot cake."

He really wants to see you, Alessandra.

"All right," I said.

He nodded. "Okay." He cleared his throat. "Eight?"

"Fine. I'll meet you there."

"Great."

Miss Cool!

I ran down the hall, where Melissa was waiting.

"I've got a date!"

Melissa screamed and held her hands to her head.

I screamed back.

Suddenly Dr. Tourneur was coming around the corner, walking with Mr. Sullivan.

"Do you girls have someplace you're supposed to be this period?"

"I'm sorry." I fumbled. "We're going to French." Melissa accidentally dropped her books. We scrambled to stuff everything into her knapsack. "I'm sorry. We're going," I kept mumbling. Dr. Tourneur stood looking at us as if we both had severe mental disorders.

We ran down the hall together and up the stairwell by the science classes. We were out of breath with trying not to laugh.

Melissa screamed again. "I can't believe it!"

"Calm down, Melissa."

"I can't help it. I'm a *jerrrrrrrk!*"

"I'm *faaaaaaat!*"

Over dinner I told my parents there was a meeting of the French club that night. (I didn't feel like being interrogated about Wyn.) My father is an engineer for Exxon. My mother is the chief officer for the firm of Stress, Panic, and Overplan.

"What kind of club has a meeting at night?" asked my father.

"They're showing a movie. A French movie."

"Really?" asked my mother.

"Some Truffaut film. I forget the title."

"I love Truffaut," said my mother. "Would they let us come? We're not doing anything tonight, are we, Ted?"

"You have to be a member of the club," I said.

"We could pay some kind of fee. I'm sure they wouldn't turn us away."

"Sure," said my father. "We'd pay a couple of bucks to see it. I think I hear your phone, Alessandra."

I ran to my room, knowing it was Wyn about to cancel.

It was Melissa. She was doing her rich-girl voice. "So, Alessandra, like, I'm so depressed about your date. It's, like, we're never going to see each other anymore, right?"

"So, Melissa, it's, like, *one* date."

"So, Alessandra, like, *everything* in my life is falling apart, right? Like, the Jacuzzi's broken. Like, I'm mega-bummed."

"Which Jacuzzi? The one in the living room or the one in the bedroom?"

"The one in the laundry room. God, Alessandra, you're so gauche. So when are you meeting him?"

"Eight, she said casually. It's all extremely casual."

"You? *Casual?*"

"Well, I've been swallowing birth control pills all afternoon to try and make up for sixteen years of not taking them, but other than that everything's extremely casual. Listen, they're calling me for dinner."

"I demand the full story, Alessandra."

"Filled with every inappropriate detail?"

"You can skip all the appropriate ones."

"You got it!"

I bounced back to the kitchen.

"Sorry."

"Next time tell your friends you're eating."

"It was Melissa; she's difficult to hang up on."

"Is she going to the film as well?"

"—The film, yes, she is. I'm going to meet her there."

"Your father and I have decided to stay in tonight. I'm tired."

"That's too bad; I think you would have enjoyed it."

My mother looked at the clock. "When is it again? Maybe we could see part of it."

"Oh, you wouldn't like it," I said, dropping my knife. "Usually the projector breaks down. It's always a disaster. I only go because my friends are there."

"You want a lift?" asked my father. "I can give you and Melissa a ride over. It's cold."

"Thanks anyway." I tried to get up and nearly spilled everything on the floor.

"What's the matter, Alessandra?"

"I'm nervous."

"What about?"

"You know me; I'm always nervous. I'm surprised my hair hasn't turned gray."

I spent an excessive amount of time in the shower. I found a radio station playing the Bards of Passion, and the music rocked the tiny room—*Surrender your love to the windfall light/Shed no bitter tears tonight/Sing, my heart/Sing, my heart*—until my father beat on the door for me to turn it down. I tried not to think about the evening; it made me too nervous. I was happy. Sometimes I'm afraid of happiness; it's too airy, too tantalizing. But for those few minutes in the shower I let happiness wash over me, let it roll down my spine and sparkle, caress me and make me glow. My whole body was warm with it. I might have been six years old. There was no school, there were no parents, there were no grades—just pure steaming water. I was Alessandra F. Hogarth, feet firm on the ground, the girl with a date!

Sing, my heart.

I hot-combed my hair and talked to Melissa on the phone while I worked elaborately on my nails.

"I'm just amazed, Alessandra. A date. I never thought this would happen. It's one thing to talk to this guy in school. There are plenty of guys I talk to in school, but—"

"Really? Who?"

"There are *hundreds* of them, Alessandra. I talk to many guys."

"When does this happen? When I'm not looking? Name one."

"I talked to Mr. Melrose in study hall today. The study hall you wish you had."

"And what did he say to you?"

"He looked into the limpid pools of my eyes—"

"Good vocabulary word."

"—and he said, 'Melissa, can you go around with a

34

garbage can and help me clean out these desks?' "

"God, I wish I'd been there. But let's get to the big question, Mel. What am I going to wear?"

"That's the big question?"

I held my head in my hands. "Life is so hard, isn't it?"

"I've got it," said Melissa. "The hiking boots with the purple laces, the argyle socks (they've got a little purple in them,) the painter's pants—"

"They don't fit anymore."

"Okay, then the jeans with the snaps at the ankles, that black-and-purple urban-guerilla pullover you like, the red sunglasses with the checkerboard frames, the feather boa, your father's Air Force wings, and your purple beret."

"I don't know about the Air Force wings," I said. "They might clash."

Talking with Melissa was a good way to calm my nerves. I liked Mel's idea of the black-and-purple urban-guerilla pullover; it was one of my favorite pieces of clothing. I especially liked that all the openings had drawstrings. Okay, red socks for good luck. The jeans with the snaps, and red sneakers for more good luck. My plastic fruit necklace; he thought that was funny. And just enough fragrance to anesthetize him into liking me!

Four

The wind was blowing and most of the snow had melted in the rain. It felt more like fall than January. I watched my breath steam and smiled. I sang to myself, *"Seems she forgot all about the French movie/Like she told her old man, now."*

It was about a twenty-minute walk to the diner. As I ambled along in the dark, I was thinking about dating. What a crazy, wonderful ritual! I started composing a personal ad for myself in my head:

> Neurotic but likable 16-yr.-old temptress with long, red hair seeks young Marlon Brando type for exotic walks to mailbox. Musician preferred. Throb preferred even more.

As I got near the diner, I tried to memorize the details of the walk. Your first date, Alessandra. Welcome to the real world. I studied the silhouettes of the winter trees under the streetlamps. Whenever you see trees like this, I thought, lonely winter pines, their arms in rags of snow, you'll remember the night of your first date. It seemed a suitably romantic thought.

North Avenue lay ahead. I could hear the swishing of the car tires. The streetlights changed from soft yellow to an ugly pink.

The parking lot of the diner was nearly full. A boy in a white apron loaded trash into a garbage bin. He let the lid smash shut; the noise made me wince.

Relax. It's a date. That's all it is.

Then why did I want more than anything in the world to be home, hanging around with Melissa?

I wanted to be warm.

I looked around those dark streets thinking: How in the world, Alessandra, did you end up in some remote corner of northern New Jersey, your nose dripping, your feet cold, standing by a diner at eight o'clock on a Friday night, scared to meet a boy a year older than you?

You have to be extremely cool tonight, Alessandra. You're young and foolish and probably in love, but keep your feet on the ground. Be careful. Be brave.

I saw his van in the lot, and I looked up to see him waiting in the glassed-in entrance room. He was leaning back against a video game with his arms folded. He saw me and smiled.

"You look good," he said. "All rose colored from the wind."

"I walked."

"A cold night for that. I was starting to wonder if you were going to show."

"Do you really think I'd do that to you?"

"I don't know," he said. "This whole thing feels kind of weird to me. I guess I'm not used to it."

"You mean you're not out picking up junior girls every Friday night?"

"I usually try to stick to alternate Fridays."

"I'm glad I got you on an odd night."

He opened the door for me.

"Thank you, kind chauvinist."

We walked past some tables and found an empty booth by the windows.

"Here. I bought you a present," he said. He seemed extremely nervous. He fumbled with a paper bag. "It took me a long time to find a present that I felt really captured your sensitivity and intelligence."

"Sounds boring."

38

"Oh, it's worse than that. It's cute."

Inside the bag was a stuffed monkey. It was one of those long thin ones that grandmothers make out of old socks. It had a sweet face.

"I love it," I said.

Wyn was happy. "I saw it this afternoon in town, and I said: 'That's for Alessandra.'"

"Now I wish I'd brought you something."

"You didn't? Okay, I'm going."

I set the stuffed monkey (Wyn explained that his name was Mr. Boo-boo—accent on the second "boo") on the table, leaning back against the wall. Wyn was dressed as he'd been at school, but he was wound up. He talked incessantly about movies and music. He took a napkin and held it between his fingers to flip the selections on the jukebox. "I'm too neurotic to actually touch the machine," he said.

"You're crazy."

"So are you, Alessandra. That's why I like you. Most of the people in that school make me sick. They're all exactly the same, with their crewneck sweaters. Just like at Millburn. They're all right out of the same stamper, you know? They *smile* too much. It makes me nervous. All money and no talent. They'll end up going to school in Boston, majoring in business administration. They'll come home on weekends and talk about how drunk they got. This is one crummy jukebox."

We kept pumping quarters into the machine. I did most of the choosing—the Bards of Passion, of course. I tried to get him enthusiastic about the songs, but he just listened politely and remarked that they were "interesting."

" 'Interesting' is all you can say about Throb?"

He listened for a moment. "Okay. Interesting and boring."

"Boring?"

"First of all, it's hard for me to get serious about a guy named Throb. Second, it's the same chord changes over and over again. It's boring."

"Excuse me," I said, sipping my tea. "It's not boring; it's mesmerizing; it's hypnotic."

"No wonder I'm falling asleep."

I gave him a mock scowl. "Throb used to be an English teacher. His lyrics contain references to John Keats and Dylan Thomas."

"Yeah, but can you dance to it?" He smiled his goofy grin. "You have to forgive me, Alessandra. I don't listen to that much pop music."

"That's why I'm trying to educate you." I thought for a moment. "How about if we make each other cassettes? We each take an hour cassette and fill it

40

with music we love. Then we'll exchange them. What do you say? Would you do that?"

"Sounds pretty interesting."

"I'll give you the Bards of Passion and all my favorite stuff. Then you give me, you know, Yo-Yo Ma—or whatever you listen to."

"So you get the Brahms Trios and I get Throb. That sounds fair."

As he said it, I knew it would never happen. He shook the little packets of sugar furiously and poured them into his black coffee. Up close there was something appealingly sharp and angular in his face. He was talking again about music, and I kept asking myself: What's really going on inside him?

"—and that's sort of funny, really, since he actually studied under Leonard Rose in the early sixties, but I think Rose is a hundred times better. On a certain level, the Yo-Yo Ma records are just plain boring."

"Like Throb?"

"Well, you look up boring in the dictionary and they've got a picture of Throb."

I was thinking: Am I smart enough to keep up with this guy?

"Do you think you'll be famous, Wyn?"

I meant the question sort of casually, but it stopped him cold. I continued: "Will I be able to say that I knew you when you used to eat toasted bagels in the Westfield Diner, and you were too scared to touch the jukebox?"

"And how much I hated Throb?"

"Hey, I have enough discretion to leave that out. I don't want you coming off as a total idiot."

"That's reassuring."

"You can always count on me for good taste," I said.

He smiled. "The first time I saw you, Alessandra, you had a fox piece around your neck with the little paws still attached; you had a gold stick-on star on your cheek, and you were wearing a huge red hat."

"Tasteful, huh?"

"That's one word for it."

"Hey, you said you were sick of the crewneck sweaters."

"But you went right from L.L. Bean to Ringling Brothers."

"And how about you? Mr. Black Shirt and Tan Pants? If somebody dies in this restaurant, you'll be the only one who's dressed for it."

He seemed genuinely pleased to be exchanging barbs with me. We both were being loud and theatrical. In truth, there was something of a performance about the night. My heart was racing. I was sweating. We were trying hard to impress each other. And I thought: He likes me. It was nothing short of amazing.

"I asked you before if you thought you'd be famous," I said. I was trying to slow down a little. I tried breathing deeply.

He rubbed his eyes. "I can't really answer that."

"Why not?"

"It's too . . . I don't know."

"What?"

He looked at the cars outside the window. "How can you answer a question like that? It's like asking somebody, What do you really want out of life? How can you answer that and not seem foolish?"

"You can ask me."

"Okay, Alessandra, what do you really want out of life?"

I looked him right in the eye. "I want to create one thing that is unassailably beautiful."

He looked seriously back at me. "That's a good answer."

"I've been waiting sixteen years for somebody to ask me that question. I was ready."

He smiled. "You're very special, Alessandra." He

shook his head. "I don't know what planet you come from."

"The planet Deeply Neurotic. The constellation Hopelessly Confused."

He asked me about the flute.

"I've been taking lessons since I was in elementary school."

"Are you good?" He gulped another coffee. I sipped my tea.

"It gives me pleasure. There's some real—I don't know—truth in music. Even rock music."

"Something unassailably beautiful in rock music?" he said.

"Maybe. I listen to lots of things, anyway. Even classical, heaven help me. Music spooks me sometimes. It's as if you're not listening to the music anymore. You're listening through the music, listening to something secret. Something you could never tell anyone. Some paintings affect me like that, too."

"What paintings do you like?"

He asked me the question seriously, but there was something in his tone that suggested he didn't care.

"I love Van Gogh," I said.

"Would you play the flute for me sometime?"

"No. I'd be too self-conscious."

"I'd love to hear you."

"Well, if I asked you to play the cello for me, would you do it?"

"Yes."

I smiled. "Well, you see, you're one of those people who were born to perform at Juilliard, and I'm one of those people who were born to perform in her bedroom."

"I'd still love to hear you."

"*Love* to hear me—or *like* to hear me? Mr. Melrose says you shouldn't use the word 'love' indiscriminately."

"You love that English teacher, don't you?"

"I like him."

"Okay, I'd *like* to hear you play."

"Maybe—" A crazy thought crossed my mind. "I just had an idea that maybe I could perform at the next music masters recital . . . but I think I'd probably be too nervous."

"That'd be a great place to hear you."

I laughed. "Maybe."

"When's the next one?"

For some reason I was suddenly shaking. "Well, if I did it, it'd be in about three weeks."

"Great. Your tea is getting cold."

I excused myself to go to the bathroom. I needed time to think. I was burning. I opened the window. It was raining outside now; the water looked pink under the arc lamps. I loosened my collar and tried to calm down.

Why was I on fire like this? I was bored, actually, by a lot of his conversation. He seemed completely self-absorbed. Did he really like me? Or did he just want me to like him? To give him an audience for all that ambition? And what about his other girlfriend— the one he was dancing with? Wasn't I going to ask about her?

As I returned to the table, he was flipping through the jukebox again. There was my empty coat across from him. I laughed out loud. It looked so much like a couple!

Get up your confidence, I thought.

I plumped myself down. "So about this girl you were dancing with the other night?" I folded my hands demurely and stared at him. I felt as if I had a fever.

He looked at me. "She's my friend. Debbie."

"Your friend?"

"Yes, she goes to Millburn High."

"Is she your girlfriend-friend?"

"She's a friend."

"Would you have told me about her if I hadn't asked?"

"I don't know," he answered quickly and, I thought, truthfully. He studied the jukebox.

"What's her last name?"

"Pappas."

I nodded silently, my inner tape recorder glowing red, taking it all in.

"Her father's my family doctor."

I nodded again.

"It was nice to have a place to escape to when things got ugly at home," he said. "My parents separated a couple of months ago. A decision they should have made three years before that. That's why we moved from Millburn."

"I'm sorry about your parents."

"There's nothing to be sorry about. I think everybody's happier now." He shrugged as if to say: Enough about this.

"I'm still curious about Debbie."

"I can see that."

"Well, I saw you dancing with her."

He smiled—then his face grew serious. "There was a time in my life when I was in love with her. I'm not any longer. It's taken me a long time to be able to say that. Things were very intense for a while; I don't think it was making either of us happy. I used to drive home from her house saying to myself, 'Who needs this?'—which sounds callous and awful, I know."

"What was the matter?"

"I don't know. She needed somebody to take care of her. I couldn't handle it. I wanted to help her; I really did. For a long time I tried, but I just couldn't keep putting myself through the emotional wringer. I'd leave my house, where I thought somebody was ready to kill from all the tension. Then I'd hit her house and all her problems. I used to walk back to the van, and just collapse on the front seat and say, 'I can't handle this.'" He tried to smile. "Did you ever have a relationship like that?"

I shook my head. Suddenly I felt much younger than he was.

"So I'm not looking for any more heavy-duty intensity, okay? I need a little rest. I could also use a few laughs."

"So you're exploiting me purely for my entertainment value?"

"Do you mind?"

"Exploit away," I said.

He drained his coffee. "And that's the story on Debbie Pappas."

"I appreciate your being honest with me."

"Why don't you tell me about *your* love life?" he asked.

"Oh, sailors mostly. Football players. I like guys with tattoos."

"Me too."

We talked for about thirty minutes more. The mood was light, but I was glad I had asked about Debbie. I tried to remember her from the dance: her curly hair, her beautiful shoulders. I wondered how they'd met. I wondered if they had slept together. The question suddenly seemed of absolute importance to me. *There was a time in my life when I was in love with her.* Surely that meant that they had. But when had it happened? Did she love his eyes? I imagined her unbuttoning that black short-sleeved shirt, to touch her hand to that pale skin.

He drove me home in the van. It was fun to be riding so high with the stiff springs clanging below us. I kept thinking, I'm in his van. It was ridiculous to be so happy about something so insignificant. But I was happy. His cassette machine played Bach's Cello Suite #1 in G Major. It was chilling music— beautiful to the bone. As it spun its netting over me, I felt that Wyn was somehow connected to it, that he had participated in its creation.

He pulled up in front of my driveway. "Fancy dump," he said.

"Not my style of house," I said. "In San Diego we lived in this old Queen Anne with a turret. I loved that house. It had this great, dark winding wooden staircase that came right down to the front door. I can still smell the wood. I have this dream that someday when I make a lot of money, I'm going to buy it."

"I'm sure someday you will," he said. "And now I think this is the part where I walk you to your door and we shake hands."

"We can shake hands here, I think."

He took my hand across the dark front seat. "Good night, Alessandra." Then he intoned dramatically: "So am I going to see you again?"

"I don't know," I said. "I'm just looking for a few laughs."

I waved good-bye as his van turned toward Lawrence Avenue. "And that was the last I ever saw of him," I said aloud. My pale cellist. I sighed. I sat for a while on the curb to collect my thoughts. I'd seen too many movies. My nose was dripping, and I hoped I wasn't getting a cold. I had to go to the bathroom, too. ("Alessandra, you're so *human*," Melissa always says.)

I looked at my house, ablaze in its awful one-floor, high-tech opulence. I didn't have the stomach to go inside yet. In my old house I'd had the entire third floor to myself. I was nourished by that house. It had given me the most private sense of who I was. I re-membered when I was Alessandra of Green Gables, inventing adventures in my head.

And here I was. Sitting with a stuffed monkey on a curb in New Jersey. Sighing about some guy. I laughed. How the mighty had fallen!

Five

Melissa and I had an interesting day in New York last week. We went in to buy Wyn a birthday present. I wore my black vampire dress, and Melissa wore her pale-yellow St. Tropez Marina sweatshirt. It has silver lettering that matches the silver lenses of her sunglasses.

New York is a wild place. Melissa hates it because of all the weird people, but I enjoy them. Along with my black vampire dress, I wore my cat-woman leather boots and a leopard-spotted shawl. This anemic-looking guy with thick glasses and a receding hairline tried to pick me up in the subway station. He walked up to me and said, "You have got *remarkably* red hair."

"Thank you."

"I once had a girlfriend with long red hair like that."

Meanwhile, Melissa is pulling at my sleeve. "We have to go, Alessandra. We have to go *now*." She finally manages to drag me away. "What are you doing, Alessandra? Some pervert is trying to pick you up and you're talking to him."

"What can I tell you? I'm attractive to perverts."

We took the subway down to the Village to find a present for Wyn. He's a Pisces; I'm a Virgo: the two most romantically incompatible signs in the zodiac. The virgin and the sturgeon!

We wandered around West Fourth Street looking for an appropriate present.

"I don't know why you want to get him any-thing," said Melissa. "He already has a girlfriend. And please don't tell me again how she's only his 'friend.' "

"I like him. I know that is a concept beyond the scope of your depraved understanding. Occasionally you can just like someone, and not be madly, passion-ately in love with him."

"But you *are* madly, passionately in love with him."

"What does that have to do with anything?"

"Alessandra, you're sick. Deeply, deeply sick. I think you need serious professional care."

"Thank you, Doctor Silverman."

"Well, you're only in love with a guy who announces to you, I mean he comes right out and *announces* to you, that he has a girlfriend. That he just wants to be friends."

"I only want to be friends, too. Friends who sleep together."

I saw these great earrings made from green plastic dinosaurs. They were big brontosauruses that hung from your ears by the tails. They were outrageously expensive, so I begged Melissa to buy them for me, but she, as usual, dismissed my longing for exquisite jewelry as a sign of superficiality.

"You're so deep, Alessandra," she said. "So deep."

We stopped in front of the Chez Decadence Boutique and examined the merchandise in the window.

"Do you think he'd like edible underwear?" asked Melissa.

"I bought him that last week."

We finally bought him a memo pad with piano keys

printed in the margin. I wanted to buy him an inflatable woman, but Melissa felt it was in poor taste.

We spent the rest of the afternoon walking in circles around a porno movie theater with Melissa insisting that we try to get in. We must have walked around the block ten times.

"They're going to ask for I.D.'s, Melissa."

"No, they're not. This is New York. They don't ask for anything."

"And what if they do ask?"

"They won't, Alessandra. God, you're so immature."

"*I'm* immature? Why don't *you* buy the tickets?"

"I don't look eighteen!"

We walked around the block one more time.

"Look," said Melissa. "You want to see one of these pictures, don't you?"

"You're the one who's dying to see it."

"Now, Alessandra, come on. You've got to think of it as educational."

"Educational?"

"Yes . . ." She held her hand out expressively. "It's sort of an extension of Family Health."

"Oh, Melissa, you're sick."

"Look, here it is. What do you have to do? You walk

up to the woman and you say, 'When is the next show?' And then you say, 'Okay, I'd like two tickets.' "

"The woman is staring at us. We've walked by twenty times. She's probably calling the police."

"Come on, Alessandra! Listen, this'll count as my birthday present, okay?"

The film was *Astral Bodies*. A blue banner was strung beneath the marquee. In gold lettering it read: *The Biggest Bosoms in the Universe.*

"Come on, Alessandra. For me."

"Oh, God," I said.

Gathering all my courage, I headed alone toward the box office.

There was a girl in her twenties behind the glass. She was listening to a tape player with headphones. On one side of the window it said *Admission $5.00.* Beneath was a sign: *No one admitted under the age of 18. Proof required.* I adjusted my leopard-spotted shawl. Okay, think twenty, Alessandra. Think adult.

"What time is the next show?" I asked, my voice cracking.

She looked directly at me. "Two thirty."

I nodded a few times. "Okay . . . thanks very much."

I walked calmly back to Melissa.

Then we laughed like maniacs, ran down the street, and took the next train home.

He liked the notepad. I gave it to him the other day when he took me out for a pizza. That entire afternoon turned out to be an amusing sort of disaster. He was irritated that I could make any restaurant table look like a war zone in about five seconds. We were waiting for the pizza. His side of the table was immaculate. My side was littered with ten straw wrappers, twenty crumpled napkins, and a pound and a half of spilled salt and pepper. Then, in my extravagant nervousness, I spilled my can of ginger ale all over the table. Even Wyn couldn't help laughing.

I was fast and funny that day. I was flying. Wyn dropped me off at my house, and I immediately went out for a forty-minute walk—all the way to Brightwood Park and back. It was a gloriously sunny afternoon. I watched a lady playing with her dog in a field. When I got home, I felt as if I had twice as much energy as when I'd started.

He called me later that night and we ended up arguing. I was trying to convince him to go to the Cupid Computer dance with me, but he had planned to attend a concert.

"I'm sorry, Alessandra. I can't miss this."

"Could I go with you?"

"I don't have another ticket. I'm somebody else's guest."

"Whose? Debbie's?"

"Her father has tickets at Carnegie Hall."

"So bring me along. Say, 'Debbie, I'd like you to meet Alessandra, the girl I'm living with.'"

There was a silence.

"Hellooooooo!" I said spiritedly. "Hello, Wyn–darling–honey–sweetie. Are you still there, my little poison bottle?"

"Yes, my little iron maiden."

I'm writing in black, which means I'm not in a good mood. I don't know what to make of my "friendship" with Wyn. It's funny when he and I are together, because there's one part of me that wants to be close to him and another part that tells me nothing is going to come of this relationship. (Is there a worse word in the English language than "relationship"?)

We went out bike riding yesterday, which started all right and ended miserably. First, we rode to town and had lunch together. It annoys him no end that I order things from the menu by pointing to the pictures. "I'll have one of those," I say, tapping my fingernail on some Technicolor fantasy of a clam platter.

"Alessandra, Alessandra . . ." he says. "You know you're getting ripped off. You're being manipulated by the cheapest kind of marketing. You're ordering the most expensive things on the menu."

I do my small-and-forlorn look while he lectures me. I crumple some napkins. Then when the waitress comes around for dessert, I say, "Give me one of those!" pointing to a garish picture of a sundae with a Hershey bar sticking out the top.

Wyn. Wyn. Wyn. Over the last week, we've seen each other with some regularity—all light, noncommital kinds of dates: ice cream, the library, a drive on Route 22 to buy him some blank cassettes.

There are times when I am filled with genuine affection for him, and often much more than that. He took me to dinner the other night at the tavern in Morris Plains. The place was so crowded that we had to sit at the bar. It was wonderful. The jukebox was playing the Bards of Passion, and the silverware was jangling, and the hostess was calling over the loudspeaker, "Number seven, party of five, upstairs." My steak was delicious and my tea burned inside me. Wyn and I seemed not to run out of conversation. He

59

had bought me a present: the single of Throb's "Lone Writer of the Purple Prose." We laughed about the song. The single was pressed on purple vinyl, and everybody at the bar wanted to check it out. The whole evening was a celebration. I held Wyn's hand, and I didn't want to be anywhere else on earth.

But the evening ended with an argument. During the drive home, I said I wanted to watch a movie on television. He said that he didn't like television; it gave him a headache.

"But you go ahead and watch it," he added. "I want to head home anyway."

"I wanted to watch the movie with you."

"I told you, television gives me a headache."

"All right, we'll do something else."

"Why don't I just go home, Alessandra? And you can watch your movie."

"Fine. Good night. Go home and practice. It's what you've wanted to do all night anyway."

"Come on—"

"Enjoy your practice. I hope it doesn't give you a headache."

I seem sometimes driven to argue with him, as if I'm deliberately trying to be destructive. Sometimes I think there must be something wrong with me.

Wyn is a curious character. On one level he's deeply cynical—he cuts down everything and everybody—and on another he seems childishly unconcerned with the world. And in the manner of a child, I don't think he realizes how much he hurts me sometimes with his indifference.

He's remote. His eyes fall back into neutral when discussing anything except music. It's only when he's on about the cello or Juilliard or the David Blair Toub scholarship that the veil really lifts and his eyes burn and sparkle. Otherwise, he drifts along.

I'm convinced he genuinely likes me. I think I am pretty entertaining sometimes.

He also told me that I was beautiful.

Well, we biked to the park yesterday. We locked our bikes and walked through the woods. Winter had destroyed the place. It looked like the wreckage from a hurricane; strewn all around were broken limbs. The air was raw. Even the sun seemed pale and spiritless. As if to compensate for the lousy weather, we both were trying too hard to have a good time. We sat on a bench far into the woods.

"I'd sit right next to you," I said, "except I've taken the responsibility of drawing the line in this relationship." I took a felt-tip pen from my pocketbook and drew a line between us on the bench. "The line."

He smiled. "If that's what you want."

"I think it would be healthier for both of us."

"Okay."

"Well, you're still seeing Debbie, right?"

"I told you she's my friend."

"Like I'm your friend."

"After this conversation, I'm not so sure."

"Are we having a fight?"

"Why do we see each other, Alessandra, if we always end up sparring?"

"Is that what we're doing, sparring?"

"No, we're dancing."

Two squirrels chased each other around the trunk of a bare tree. Wyn took a drag on his cigarette. I coughed elaborately.

"Is my smoking bothering you?"

"Aside from the cluster headache, no."

He sighed and stared at the ground.

"The weather's just so lousy," I said. "Maybe we shouldn't have come here."

He shrugged. "Where else is there to go? My mother's at my house. There are people at your house."

"Is that why we came here? To be alone?"

"Why do you keep asking me questions like that, Alessandra?"

"I guess I like sparring. I'm freezing."

"I'd put my arm around you," he said, "except we have to draw the line."

"Yes, the line." I traced my finger across the bench. "Does Debbie know about me?"

"She knows I have a friend."

"How often do you see her?"

"Come on, Alessandra."

"Do you see her more than you see me?"

"Let's change the subject, all right?"

"Right. Let's talk about El Salvador," I said. "Personally, I say, 'Hands off.'"

He looked up at the trees. "I want to kiss you," he said. "I've wanted to all afternoon. I just thought it was stupid of me to be sitting here thinking this and not tell you."

"Do you kiss Debbie?"

"No one on earth would believe this conversation."

I was playing with my scarf. I looked up at him. "All right, Wyn," I said. "One kiss. But it doesn't mean anything. Only one and we still haven't crossed the line, okay?"

"Okay," he said. "One brief, insignificant kiss."

My heart was going like crazy. He bent over and gave me a kiss. I sat there thinking, Okay, sweet sixteen and I've been kissed.

"That's it," he said. "Okay? Give me the pen." He took it and retraced the line on the bench. "The line is intact."

"The line is intact."

"Good," he said. "It's over. It's out of our systems forever. Now we can relax and be friends."

We got up and walked through some gloomy trails. He held my hand, then dropped it. "No. No. I can't do that. We have to draw the line."

"Right."

He walked ahead. Jesus, I was mixed up. Melissa kept telling me not to see him. Of course, she was right. Actually, I liked him a lot more when I didn't see him. When I was home helping my mother with the ironing, I liked to think about him. My mother would be listening to some romantic Frank Sinatra song on the radio; I'd be ironing in the laundry room, listening, and suddenly I'd find myself near tears. I'd think: God, I've got a boyfriend. He leaves me notes in my locker: "Meet you fourth period for the assembly. W." I sent him a copy of e.e. cummings' poem "if everything happens that can't be done" for Valentine's Day. It's a great love poem. Of course, I received nothing in return from him. He had to run right to New York that afternoon. So what else is new? Somehow I wouldn't have expected to receive a Valentine from him. He, of course, never made me the cassette he promised. I refuse to give him the one I made until he remembers, so it sits at home in my drawer.

When I actually see him, it's never as I imagined. It's never what I felt when I was ironing. It's misread signs and sparring and *I'm not looking for any more heavy-duty intensity.* He once told me that if it came to a choice between his music and anyone in his life, he would choose the music. He said he didn't have time for a girlfriend. . . . All this was running through my mind as we walked through that gray, broken forest.

"What's bothering you, Wyn?"

"Nothing."

"No, really, you look miles away. What are you thinking?"

"You don't want to know."

"Please."

"What I was thinking was a profound violation of the line."

We walked for a while.

"I'm sorry," he said. "You asked."

We bicycled back through town. The sky was darkening. My ears hurt from the cold, and my nose was dripping.

"Should I come in for a while?" he asked in front of my house.

"No. I have to practice. I'm playing in the music masters in a week."

"I'll be there."

"I'm not that good."

"I'll see you at school, Alessandra."

"Is that a question?"

He looked so handsome standing there. His face was red with the cold. His brown hair was wild from the wind. He stood in the dusk in his camel's-hair coat and blue scarf.

"I apologize for this afternoon," he said.

"You don't have to apologize."

"I do like you, Alessandra."

"And I like you," I said. But a voice inside me said: *No, I don't. I just want to fall in love so much I'm pretending.*

I talked about it that night with Melissa.

"He *does* like me, Mel. Sometimes he really does."

"Anything you say, Alessandra."

"He said to me once that he thought I was beautiful."

66

"That means you have big breasts."

"He said that he admired my 'intelligence and vitality.' "

"That means you have *really* big breasts."

Six

Melissa's parents are in Europe. They've left her in the hands of her older sister, Robin. I've spent the afternoon over there—books spread all over the kitchen table. It's good to do work in the kitchen because you can stop and eat every few seconds.

Mel's sister Robin is twenty-two, pretty, and hip. She works in New York. She gave us a ride into Millburn this morning. It was an expedition of inspired detective work. Wyn had told me that Debbie's father was a doctor, and sure enough, in the Suburban Essex directory there were two phone numbers listed for a Stanley Pappas, M.D. One address was on Old Short Hills Road; the other was on Wildrose Drive. We had to figure out which address was his practice and which was his home. Melissa went flipping through the yellow pages.

We finally found the elusive Stanley Pappas, M.D., on Old Short Hills Road. This meant his residence was on Wildrose Drive. I was dying to see what Debbie's house looked like.

Robin agreed to drive us to Millburn.

The street was almost at the top of a mountain. The beautiful old homes had ended, and we drove through hideous, treeless construction sites. We made the turn onto Wildrose, and the houses were even worse: monstrous, bloated boxes with Mercedes convertibles parked in the arcs of the driveways.

"The people in this neighborhood," said Robin, "have too much money and too little taste."

It was a short, stunted street. There wasn't a tree in sight, only walls of shrubs cut to look like traffic cones. My eyes scanned to the end of the block, and in a second I saw it. "That's his van," I said.

Wyn's pale-blue van was parked in front of the last house on the left. It stood modestly in the winter sun, the only curbside automobile on the street.

Debbie's house was a grotesque testament to affluence: white, three-storied, lattice-windowed, with a chandelier hanging over the main entrance. All was still. The shades were drawn. It looked as if there was no one home except Wyn and Debbie.

"Are you satisfied?" asked Robin.

"His *ex*-girlfriend?" said Melissa.

Robin turned around to look at me. "You want a piece of advice?"

"No."

"Find yourself somebody else."

"Are you kidding?" said Melissa. "This is her big romance, which is going to stand the test of time."

"What time *is* it?" I said, looking at my watch.

"Take my advice," said Robin. "Find somebody else."

I've unplugged the phone. I have spent two days crying.

Every couple of Wednesdays the music department has its after-school music masters recital in which students play or sing to friends, teachers, and parents. It's a small showcase. Usually I would be too nervous even to consider it, but I had this idea that I wanted to prove something to Wyn. I wanted to prove I was good at something creative. I thought he might like me more.

Mrs. Gerber, the school music teacher, and I had been working on a flute-and-piano duet—a short adaptation from the Mozart Flute Concerto in D—and she thought it was good enough to be performed. Mrs. Gerber seems sure of herself; after you talk to her for a while you begin to feel sure of yourself, too. It's got something to do with her humor—the ease with which she dismisses problems, her constant willingness to be sympathetic. It all seems to be saying to you, "Relax. Life is bearable and funny." I suppose that's why she always has students hanging around her.

I agreed to play at the next music masters. My name was written on the sign-up sheet by the door. I had made a commitment.

We practiced in the chorus room after school. I insisted, though, that she close the doors so no one could watch. I like the chorus room, especially in the late afternoon with the sunlight soft on its wooden floors. I like the worn chairs, the battered music stands tumbled against the back wall, the filing cabinets stuffed with old marching music. The old black Steinway sits on its large wheels in the middle of the room. It's slightly out of tune, and the low D sticks, but it's got character. It's easy to imagine the thousands of students who must have played it. My flute sounds great in the chorus room. Without amplification it sounds full.

We practiced with a humorous diligence. I stood in my faded denim dress, watching my reflection in the brass flower bowl on top of the piano.

"Let's pick it up from 32," she'd say. "And watch the tempo change; you're getting fast."

I nodded. I rarely said anything during practice. I liked not using my voice. It made the music sound holier.

After a week we felt we were as ready as we were ever going to be. But the recital was canceled once, then canceled again because of a conflict with standardized testing. There was a great deal of yelling about the cancelations, and threats to eliminate the whole program if nobody thought it was important enough. But at last it all came together. That Wednesday in Unified Math, we heard the morning announcements over the speaker, and my name was there. I saved the ditto: *All students and faculty are invited to attend the music masters recital today in the chorus room at three p.m. Refreshments will be served. Performing will be some of our most talented young musicians, among them David Shen, Kim Elzinga, the Four Juniors, and Alessandra Hogarth. Everyone is welcome. The program will begin promptly at three.*

When the announcement was read, I was both embarrassed and proud. Some people in the class gave me a hand. I thought about my name being heard in all the rooms throughout the school.

I was, of course, too nervous to even think about eating lunch that day. Throughout the afternoon I sat in my classes, lost. I had a dull headache and a ringing in my ears. I sat through French with my eyes shut. I kept hearing the music in my head. I thought, somehow, that if I imagined a perfect performance, heard every perfect note, then when it actually came time to play, my fingers would remember, and the performance would be flawless.

I spent study hall in the library. I was too nervous to read anything serious. I looked up my horoscope in the newspaper. *Virgo: Self-doubt is your bugaboo now.*

Melissa reminded Wyn about my performance. She also reminded Mr. Melrose.

The day ticked on relentlessly. Every time I looked at the clock, I felt so sick I couldn't speak. Gym was a nightmare. We did calisthenics, and I felt that any moment I was going to throw up. Sit-ups, running in place, push-ups. I was turning green. Thirty bodies sweated and pounded on the floor.

The day ended with history, my worst class. There was a "lightning notebook review." Ms. Haboush shoots out questions, then calls on whoever finds the answer first. You get extra credit for every correct answer. With the clock over her head telling me *how soon*, it was all I could do to keep from passing out. But I kept flipping madly through my notebook, pretending I was looking for the answer. The class was loud and uncontrolled. *Unfair,* they kept yelling. *I had my hand up first.*

I asked permission to go to the bathroom.

"Can't it wait?"

"No," I said.

"All right," she said, as if she were doing me some enormous favor. "Take the pass."

The bell rang. I felt as if I had food poisoning. There was a dead heaviness in my face. *Self-doubt is your bugaboo now.* I wanted to run away from that school. I wanted to tell Mrs. Gerber I was too sick to play. But I also knew I had to force myself to go through with it.

Kim Elzinga stopped me in the hall and asked if I was nervous.

"Yes."

"I'm dying," she said. She held her stomach and grimaced.

I liked her for that. I liked her for her braids and her shortness and her honesty.

The hall was full of people. Most were on their way home. I descended the chorus room stairs, deliberately feeling each hard step. Inside, the room was filled with noise and the smell of brownies. Four students were banging on the piano, playing something from the school play, *Godspell.*

"Alessandra," a voice called over my shoulder.

It was my mother. Parents often came to the music masters, but I honestly hadn't expected her to appear.

"You didn't have to come, Mom."

"I wanted to hear you."

She was dressed for work—a long, tan cashmere dress with a cowl neck. I was glad to see her.

"You don't look so good," she said.

"I'm nervous."

"Just pretend everybody in the audience has no clothes on."

I gave her a smile. "That's what I always pretend."

Perlmacher was gesturing for everyone to take a seat. I sat by my mother. Melissa sat next to me.

"I want to start, if everybody will take a seat," said Perlmacher. People were eating brownies from the refreshment table. "Those are for afterward," he said. "Please let's all be seated."

Wyn was there, sitting by himself in the back row, up by the windows. He waved to me. I smiled and looked away. Melissa put her arm on mine. "Melrose is here," she said.

He came hurrying through the door, carrying his attaché case and a stack of folders.

Perlmacher made a brief introduction and the recital began. It was already twenty after three.

David Shen started with a solo violin piece, and in five seconds everybody in the room knew it was going to be endless. He is a small, dark-haired boy, and he plays with a frightening intensity, but the piece was just too hard for him. It was sad. The mistakes were loud and graceless.

"He stinks," Melissa whispered to me.

I watched Melrose in the back row with the sun pouring through his brown hair. I watched Wyn sitting with his hands over his eyes, as if he were hiding from the music.

I made no comment. I dared not.

When David was through, the audience applauded loudly. I was glad. He bowed shyly and took his seat.

The Four Juniors were next. They were always popular with the crowd. In fact, most of the audience were other members of the *Godspell* cast, and there was all sorts of cheering when they appeared. The four girls were poised and relaxed. Susan took her place at the piano and played the opening line of "Swanee River." This got an enormous laugh from the *Godspell* cast. Sara stood with her hands in the pockets of her dress, looking directly at the audience. She announced, "This is an original song entitled 'The Widows of War.' The words are by Kristin and myself. The music is by Susan."

They performed with great clarity and presence, and at the song's conclusion they were met with enormous applause. They left the room immediately to attend the *Godspell* rehearsal. Many audience members left with them.

Now the only performers remaining were Kim Elzinga and myself. My flute was hot in my shaking hands. Across the room I could see Mrs. Gerber checking her piano score. Wyn reread his program. I was after Kim. I retied the laces on my shoes as tightly as I could.

Why was I ever stupid enough to have agreed to perform?

Melrose gave me a thumbs-up. I couldn't even smile.

Kim played some thunderous Russian thing, the bass notes banging and rattling. I was struck by the incongruity of her personal quietness and the dark-souled, troubled clouds of her music. I began to study the crowd, but with a startling abruptness the piece was over. Perlmacher was announcing my name. Wyn sat up in his chair. My mother put her hand on my shoulder.

"Break a leg," she said.

I stood by the old Steinway. The room grew impossibly silent. Mrs. Gerber took a great deal of time setting up her music, fussing with and adjusting her position on the bench.

The janitor's bell rang shrilly. It took me a second to catch my breath. We tuned and I couldn't get the flute to sound right. She kept restriking the note; I adjusted the mouthpiece.

"That's good," she said.

But it wasn't exactly on pitch. I breathed deeply to calm my nerves.

She nodded.

I nodded. Wyn was sitting forward now in his chair. Mrs. Gerber began the introduction, and I stood before my music stand with an ugly headache gripping my face like fingers.

I came in too fast. I was off by a mile. We hammered away past each other for about twenty seconds. She stopped.

"From the beginning."

I nodded.

She played the introduction in a slower, more deliberate style. This time I tapped my foot to the count. But I came in wrong again, and I didn't know if I was ahead or behind. My stomach was in pieces. Don't stop, I thought. Get it over with.

The music was a horrible jumble.

She stopped. I was shaking my head. "I don't know what's wrong."

"Let's pick it up after the sixteenth notes."

I nodded.

She counted out loud and we came in together. I could feel the audience relax a little. But the count was too fast; I was slurring all the runs and squeaking. We played for about forty seconds, and it was atrocious. Just keep playing, I repeated in my mind. Let it end. Let me go home.

But she stopped again. I wanted to cry.

"A little slower . . ." she said.

She counted it in and I played as softly as I could.

We played the last three pages slowly, haltingly, as if I were a first-year music student.

The audience applauded loudly.

"I'm sorry," I said to her. I was crying. "I'm sorry.

I'm so embarrassed. I don't know what happened."

Mr. Perlmacher was thanking everybody for coming. "Let's give a big hand to all our talented young musicians."

My mother, Melissa, and Mr. Melrose were waiting when I got back from the bathroom. I was still crying. My mother kept rubbing my shoulders saying, "You were fine, Alessandra; you were fine, Alessandra."

Wyn had left.

It rained that night. I talked to Melissa on the phone. School the next day was dark and cold. The rain still beat against the windows. I fell asleep during the physics movie. It was something about the velocity of falling objects. The futility of it made me sad.

No one mentioned the recital. Then Kim Elzinga stopped by my locker. "How are you feeling?"

"Better."

"Don't worry about it, really."

She smiled at me and I wondered if she meant it. Or had they all laughed about it afterward? Had they run out to the *Godspell* people and told them, "Thank God you left when you did. It was unbelievable. We couldn't even look at her. She was so bad."

Melissa was kind. "Everybody's forgotten it already, Alessandra. It's like any audition. You think everybody else is watching you, and all they're really concerned about is themselves."

"I am so embarrassed, Mel."

"No one even remembers anymore."

I dreaded English class. Melissa had deliberately asked Melrose to attend the concert, and then I had humiliated myself. I went down to the nurse before his class to see if I had a temperature, but she said I was all right.

In obligation to my grade, I sat down just as the late bell was ringing. I had deliberately come late so I wouldn't have to talk to anyone.

He asked me a question; I mumbled some garbage for an answer. The others, the eager ones, had their hands raised instantly.

The class dragged on. Near the end we were supposed to start our homework. Reading was about the last thing in the world I wanted to do. But at least I could pretend, and I didn't have to talk to anybody. Ten minutes to go. Then I could walk home. Thank God orchestra was dropped on "A" days. I wouldn't have to face Wyn.

Melrose moved around the room, checking that people were working, and he placed a folded piece of notebook paper on my desk. I didn't read it then.

When I got home, I took a shower. I put on my flannel pajamas. I got into bed under my electric blanket. Then finally I read the note.

Alessandra:

I wanted to talk to you yesterday, but you left before I had the chance. I wanted to say that I hope you'll remember how talented you are. It's easy to lose perspective. Please don't lose faith in yourself. You're a remarkable student.
M. Melrose

Seven

I haven't written in my journal for about a week. I wish I could say that I've recovered from the music masters, but I'm still walking around with the feeling that someone's thrown acid in my face.

Wyn has been tactful about the "concert." He told me the other day that he was "grateful" I'd invited him to the performance and that my playing "grew better and better" as I went along, and that it was good to "watch me growing in confidence." There was a time in my life, I think, when I would have laughed at such courteous language. But I don't laugh anymore. I'm grateful for the attempt to make things less painful.

Wyn talked to me over lunch about a concert the Juilliard precollege orchestra is giving next Saturday night and Sunday afternoon in New York. He gave me tickets to attend both performances, but there was more than this.

"I'm going to be staying over in New York, Saturday night," he said. "My folks'll stake me for a hotel room." He smiled. "An idea crossed my mind. And if you think this is just the worst thing in the world, tell me. I thought if you wanted to—if you could somehow get away with it—that maybe we could spend the weekend together in the city."

I tapped my box of raisins reflectively. ". . . Interesting."

"I know it may just be the worst idea you've ever heard."

"When you say spend the weekend together, do you mean . . . well, I mean, define your terms."

"Whatever terms you want, Alessandra. I'm negotiable."

"I think we need a good lawyer at this table."

"If you want to just spend the day, that's fine," he said. "If you want to spend the night, that's fine, too."

"Does spend the night mean that we sleep together?"

"It means whatever you want it to mean."

I did my Ingrid Bergman voice. "Oh, Wyn, I'm so confused. You do the thinking for both of us."

He took my hand. "Of all the cafeterias in all the high schools in all the world, she had to walk into mine."

And so it went, light and sweet, and all the time I'm thinking: Okay, I can tell my parents I'm staying over at Melissa's. Her parents are still in Europe; her sister will probably cover for me. It was possible. It wasn't going to be easy, but if I genuinely wanted to, I could do it.

I talked to Melissa about it on the way home.

"No way," she said.

"You mean you won't cover for me if I want to?"

"Alessandra, you and I both know that no one on earth can stop you from doing what you want."

"So what's the problem?"

"The problem is that you and he hardly even get along with each other. We drive over to his girlfriend's house, and he's probably sleeping with her."

"So you'll cover for me, right?"

"Right."

"Could we stay at the Chelsea Hotel?" I asked Wyn by his locker. "All the poets stayed there in the twen-

85

ties and thirties. I think e.e. cummings wrote there.
And Dylan Thomas died there."

"Sounds impressive."

"Sid Vicious died there, too."

"Do they give you a special rate if you die there?"

"Could we stay there? Could we? That is, if I decide
to come."

"I guess so."

Melissa thought I was deranged. We discussed it
some more in her kitchen.

"You're going to be alone in New York in a hotel
room with him? Are you crazy, Alessandra? You'll
get arrested. I mean, you're a *minor*."

"What are they going to arrest me for?"

"I don't know," she said. "Something."

"When is an opportunity like this going to present
itself again?"

"I think you should go home and take a cold
shower, Alessandra."

"I wonder if the room will have two beds?"

"That's the least of your worries."

"It's important that I know."

"So call 'em up and ask," said Melissa.

"Oh, that's great—what do you say? 'Excuse me,
do you get two beds? I need to know because my
husband and I aren't having sex.' "

"You're going to tell them he's your husband?"

"I think you have to tell them that, don't you?"

"I don't know, Alessandra. I've never even had a boyfriend."

Now I was pacing around the kitchen. "This is driving me crazy, Mel. What would you do? If you were in my place?"

"I wouldn't be dating a senior who has another girlfriend."

"He does not have another girlfriend. He has another friend."

"Anything you say, Alessandra."

"He likes me, Mel. He genuinely does."

"And how do you feel about him?"

I stepped right in the cat's water and spilled it all over my shoes. "I think I love him." I got down on the floor and tried to wipe up the spill. I was shaking. It was the first time I had ever said anything like that aloud. I thought, this is just like me. The first time I admit I might be in love, I'm crawling around on the kitchen floor cleaning up cat food.

"When did you decide this?"

"Just now. Give me another paper towel."

"How does he feel about you?"

"I told you, Mel. He likes me."

"Does he love you?"

"Jesus, what difference does it make? Stop being so melodramatic. Get with the times, Mel, get hip. Start reading *New York* magazine, buy a condominium—then talk to me."

We laughed, and finally Melissa said, "Just tell me, what do you really want? That's all. Just tell me that."

"I don't know."

"You have to tell me your gut feeling on this, Alessandra. Do you want to go? Yes or no?"

"Yes . . . no."

"Yes or no?"

"Yes . . . no."

"That's your gut feeling now? That's your absolute, genuine gut feeling?"

"This is making me crazy!"

"Okay—call and find out about the room."

"I can't call."

"Why?"

"I'm too nervous."

"It's a telephone call, Alessandra."

"If it's so easy, then you call."

"I don't sound eighteen!"

"I'll give you ten dollars if you call, Mel."

She shook her head and touched my wrist in a motherly way. "Alessandra, you have to learn how to do these things. You're a big girl now. And when all this comes out in court, I want to be able to deny *everything.*"

I had a long talk on the phone with Wyn Thursday night. I thought it would clarify things in my head; I still wasn't convinced I was doing the right thing. I asked him to define what he wanted from the weekend.

"You like definitions, don't you, Alessandra?"

"Yes."

He thought a moment. "I think we'll have some laughs. I think we'll have a terrific time. I don't know, tell me what you want."

"I'd like to see how we get along at close quarters," I said. "See how we really feel."

"We'll have a great time. We're in this incredible city with nobody to bother us. It's freedom."

"Can we go to some movies?"

"Sure."

"And we don't *have* to sleep together?"

"I thought we agreed we'd play that by ear."

"Okay. But you're just friends with Debbie, right?"

"Alessandra—"

"And if we do fool around, Wyn, I want you to know that there is no way I'm risking getting pregnant. Do you understand that?"

"Alessandra—"

That Friday night I sat in the living room doing my homework so I wouldn't have any for the weekend. My parents were getting ready to go out.

"I'm going to sleep over Melissa's tomorrow. Is that okay?"

"Just don't forget to water the plants," said my mother.

Cool.

The next morning I bicycled over to Melissa's with my bag. The day was sunny and cold. Wyn was waiting in his van with the motor running. Melissa hugged me. "I love you, Alessandra," she said. "And call, okay? Let me know what's going on."

I said good-bye and ran to the van. I hopped into the seat as if I had always belonged there.

"You're looking good," he said.

"It's amazing what seven hours and eleven hundred dollars worth of makeup can do, isn't it?"

We didn't speak much during the ride into the city, but it was a pleasant silence. Wyn's Bach tape poured over us. I was lit with anticipation. The cold sunlight bounced around us. The van's shocks clattered over the potholes; to me it was a musical sound—bright and chaotic.

The towns passed by outside. Small things filled me with pleasure: a street sign, *No Parking When Road Is Snow Covered.* The sunlight and the company and the music came rising up around me in a way that made me want to cry. I looked at Wyn, and it felt for a moment as if we were husband and wife, as if we'd known each other for years, as if there were some graceful understanding between us in a world where loving would be easy and guiltless and renewing.

We drove over the skyway and through the tunnel. Wyn seemed nervous. He was worried that the van was going to overheat.

As soon as we got into Lower Manhattan, we searched for a gas station. We spent quite a while there; Wyn and the attendant added water to the radiator.

"I'll need a new thermostat," said Wyn as he climbed back into the van. "But it should hold for a while." He was shivering, and his beautiful hands were streaked with grease. He slapped me on the leg. "We're having a *good* time!"

We parked the van in a lot on Twenty-third Street,

and we walked toward the hotel. I could read its name against the cold blue sky. Wyn wore his long camel's-hair coat and blue scarf. Under my military topcoat I wore my gray baggies, my Jane Austen shoes (black leather with laces all the way up the front), a black oversized sweater with swirls of primary colors, a lace-collared lavender shirt, and my grandmother's pearls. He had his arm on my shoulder. A couple, I thought. All my life I had watched couples walking down city streets, and here we were!

On the corner was a grim-looking drugstore. There were metal gates over the windows.

"Wait here a second," said Wyn.

"What's the matter?"

"I forgot something." He smiled.

Indeed. I stared at my Jane Austen shoes. There was a YMCA gym across the street. A number of healthy-looking men entered carrying beach towels. I decided that someday I should exercise. I looked at my reflection in the drugstore window. I combed my hair with my fingers. My glasses made me look too bookish.

By the door of the drugstore an unshaven old man was sitting on a kitchen chair reading the *Post*. He stared at me and smiled. I turned back toward the street. The cold was creeping into my shoes.

92

My outfit suddenly seemed embarrassingly clean. I practically glowed in the sun. *Come on, Wyn.*

"All set," he said, coming out of the drugstore. He put his arm on my shoulder.

From the outside the hotel looked beautiful. It had black wrought-iron balconies that climbed straight up the front. There was a plaque outside telling of the famous artists who had lived there.

"I think," he said, "maybe you should let me go in by myself. I'll get the room, tell them a friend is joining me later. Okay?" He held my hand.

"What's the problem?" I asked.

"I don't want any hassles from them. I just don't feel like standing there, you know, the young illicit couple, while they're smiling at us behind the desk."

"I don't think it would be like that."

Once again I found myself waiting on Twenty-third Street. I took off my glasses, wiped my eyes, and walked into a magazine store.

I thought about that phrase: the young illicit couple. "Illicit" was such an old-fashioned word. A flicker of panic passed through me; my parents would kill me if they found me here.

I bought a magazine for the movie listings. The man behind the counter was reading a porno newspaper.

Little Miss Prim, I thought as I collected my change. Little Miss Prim from the suburbs.

I waited on the street.

Wyn was gone a long time again. What was the matter with him? I wanted to wash up and get warm. The creep from outside the drugstore was shuffling down the street toward the hotel.

I pulled open the lobby door and saw Wyn heading toward me. He was smiling.

"All set, lambie." He kissed me on the head.

"Can I see the room?" I asked.

"Let's eat first. The guy told me there's a great diner around here."

"I want to wash up."

"You can wash up at the diner, okay?"

"Wyn, let's hold it right here. You have to ask me things, all right? I've got a real low threshold for being ordered around."

"I'm not ordering you around."

"That's what it feels like to me."

"Look. Five seconds in New York and we're arguing."

"I'm not arguing; I'm patiently explaining."

"I love the look of patience in your eyes, Alessandra," he said. "Like patient little bayonets."

"I'm just establishing the rules."

He smiled. "The rules. I see. Like 'Let's not cross the line.'"

We headed toward the diner.

"I hate you," I said.

"I love you, too."

"What? Did I actually hear the word 'love' cross your lips? Where do I send my quarter? I want a transcript."

He put on a comically anguished voice. "You don't stop, do you? You don't stop torturing me!"

"I don't want to go to a diner, Wyn. We always go to places like that."

"I know. You want to go to some little artsy place with ferns."

"What's your problem with ferns?"

"I hate places with ferns."

"If we eat at a diner now, can we eat at my kind of place after the concert?"

"No problem."

"Why am I stupid enough to believe you?"

"Because you like me."

The City Diner turned out to be a fairly decent place—lots of ferns. There were two overhead fans that slowly revolved. Wyn was in a good mood. I stared at my cup and watched the orange tea slowly curl its color through the steaming water. I listened to him talking enthusiastically about the concert at Juilliard. He spoke of the jealousy between the first- and second-chair violinists. He said he thought if he performed well, it would help him win the David Blair Toub scholarship.

He loves to talk about himself, I thought. It was the one time he really came alive. I squeezed a slice of lemon over the tea. I liked the way the lemon juice lightened the color in a kind of magical alchemy. Sometimes when he was speaking about music, you felt the enormity of his ambition, and you felt that nothing was going to get in the way of all that talent and ego. He was the center of his own universe. He saw no further than how people affected him. He was a year older than I was, but sometimes he seemed much younger.

The lobby of the Chelsea was filled with art: blue-streaked murals, a faucet handle stuck to a canvas. It had a shabby, cast-off charm. A tiny elevator took us to the fifth floor.

From the top, looking down, I saw the curved railings of all the floors as beautiful wrought-iron ellipses. "It's like a movie," I said.

"Nice."

"Can't you feel all the ghosts in this place? All the

people who have written here? The past is all around us. You can touch it."

Wyn unlocked Room 507. "Maybe Sid Vicious died in this room."

"Would it bother you?"

"Just as long as there aren't any ferns left from the funeral."

The room was magnificent. The walls were edged in antique molding. There was a fireplace. There was even a tiny kitchen with a refrigerator that wouldn't close. The bedroom had *three* beds in it—maximum safety! The main room was a sort of artist's sitting room: a couch, broad high windows, old steam radiators.

"The guy told me that a dance company stays in this apartment," he said.

"It's beautiful. God, I want to live here the rest of my life. New York would be livable if you could come home to a place like this."

He washed up.

I sat on the window ledge. "So what movies do you want to see?"

He was wearing a powder-blue button-down shirt, drying his hands with a towel. He seemed happy. "Do you want to run out right now?"

"There's actually a postcard store in SoHo I'd like to check out. It is the best postcard store in the city."

"You want to do that right now?"

"We're in the city. We might as well exploit it."

He looked right at me. "I can think of other things we could do."

I looked right back at him. "Does Debbie know about our little weekend fling?"

"Alessandra, we've been through this."

"Does she know about me or not?"

"It's none of her business."

"And she's none of my business?"

"You know, Alessandra, let's just be nice to each other. I didn't ask you here to argue with you. Let's enjoy this weekend, okay?"

"Okay."

He kissed my hand. He hugged me.

"I want to get some air," I said.

"Is that a polite way of saying later?"

"It's a polite way of saying maybe."

We rode the elevator down.

"You know," he said, "you want to go to the post-card store. I'm not really interested in that. Could we split up and meet later for dinner? I'd like to go to the Library for the Performing Arts to listen to some records. Get psyched for the concert."

"Can I come?"

"Why don't you just find your postcard store?"

"I'd rather do something with you."

"Okay, come to the library," he said. "But don't blame me if you're bored."

"I won't be bored. But I thought you might like this postcard store. It's more like an art gallery than a store."

"Does it have ferns?"

"It's practically a greenhouse."

The ride to Lincoln Center on the subway was one of uncomfortable silence. I read the ads on the walls. He stared at the floor. I knew he didn't want me with him.

He sat there brooding. All right, I thought. Maybe if I am nothing but sweet, I can get through the barbed wire around him. Unwavering sweetness will win the day.

There was a couple sitting opposite us—arms, coats, scarves, all intermingling. They looked like college students, laughing, tugging scarves, pretending to strangle each other. They kissed about every ten seconds.

I'm sure they fought. I'm sure they sparred as much as Wyn and I, but their faces were flushed with this enormous humor and desire to be next to each other. Even if they weren't sitting together on the subway, you could have picked them out as lovers.

I imagined them while they were in school. I visualized them apart: staring out of classroom windows, thinking about one another. I know this is Romantic Scenario #21, but the truth was plain before me: They loved each other. And some part of me ached with jealousy to watch them.

I liked walking across the marble-and-cement plaza at Lincoln Center with the leaves blowing around us. You really felt in the center of a special world. I walked through the middle of a huge modern art sculpture. Wyn clanged it with his hand.

"Attractive, isn't it?" he said.

"It'll look good on the coffee table."

We entered the library, and I went to check my coat.

"You don't have to," he said.

"I'd rather not carry it."

He shrugged his shoulders. "Anything you say, Alessandra."

"Thank you, Mr. Patience."

He pointed past the gift shop to a series of listening

tables. "Here's where you can always find me when I've got time to kill in the city," he said.

He explained the layout of the three floors of the library; he showed me the magazines, the plays, the books.

About fifteen minutes later he was sitting alone, wearing headphones at a listening table, isolated in that private world he seemed determined to occupy.

I walked by a few times as I pretended to be busily looking up book titles. "Heavy date," I said to myself. I wondered why I was so hungry to want him to like me. It's pure desire, I thought. This was a case of base desire getting the best of me. And yet as much as I wanted him physically, it was desire in the abstract. When it actually came to looking him in the eyes, I felt shy.

I found a remote corner of the library and sat reading for a while. Then I stared out the window. I considered the possibility of just sneaking out on him— quietly slipping downtown and taking the bus home. How long before he would even notice? That's what was so irritating.

I found a play to read: *Five Finger Exercise.* It was well written and it killed an hour. By then the fluorescent lights in the library were giving me a headache.

I spent some time in the first-floor bathroom putting water on my face and leaning my forehead against the cold tiles. I rubbed the back of my neck. For a while I walked around outside and stood in the sunlight, trying to breathe deeply.

Upstairs, Wyn was still listening to his music. I smiled as I walked past him, but I wanted to scream: *Can't you do this on your own time? You do this every time you come to New York. I'm with you this time. It's supposed to be different.*

I said nothing. Another twenty minutes passed. I asked the man at the reference desk if he happened to have any aspirin. He didn't.

I walked over to Wyn and sat in the chair next to him. We'd been in the library about two and a half hours.

He pulled off the headphones. "Hi."

"Hi. Can we go, Wyn? This place is too hot; the lights are giving me a headache."

"Just let me hear the end of this piece," he said. "Fifteen minutes."

I said nothing.

"You didn't have to come here, Alessandra."

"I've got a bad headache. I'd like to go somewhere and get an aspirin."

102

He sighed in enormous exasperation—such a sacrifice he was making—and packed his stuff to leave.

There was a line of people at the coat check, and he smirked knowingly at his decision not to check his coat. He stood a few feet away while I waited; he drummed his fingers on the wooden wall.

"What is the big deal, Wyn? We have to wait five seconds for my coat?"

"I didn't say anything."

As we left the library, Wyn said hello to a pretty blond girl in a black body shirt.

"Another one of your girlfriends?" I asked.

"She goes to Juilliard. Plays the violin."

"She's pretty."

"She's got the worst B.O. you can imagine."

"That's really generous of you."

"I think she runs laps before she comes to practice. But she's too much of a feminist to take a shower."

"Wyn, you're the biggest misogynist I've ever met."

"Excuse me for living, but I don't know what 'misogynist' means."

"It's Greek for 'scumbag.'"

"That's very ladylike."

"I'll start acting ladylike when you start acting gentlemanlike."

"Just make sure you tell me when we're going to start acting nice to each other."

"You'll be the first to know."

I studied our reflection in the shop windows as we walked. We were a couple, but we were nothing like the girl and guy we'd seen earlier on the subway. They were in love; we were poised for a fight. Everything I did or said enraged him, and nearly everything he did or said made me furious.

I bought a little tin of six aspirins in a drugstore. I swallowed two immediately. We split the fare for a cab back to the Chelsea.

"How's your headache?" he asked after a while.

"Better."

"What do you want to do about dinner?"

"What are you in the mood for?" I asked.

"I don't care."

"I don't care either."

"Why don't we decide when we get to the hotel?"

"Okay."

He put his hand on top of mine. "I was thinking about wearing sneakers at the concert tonight. Do you think that would be funny?"

I smiled and thought: Who cares, Wyn?

I shut my eyes. It was the same story. Talk about me, Alessandra. Ask questions about me. Pretend I'm famous. The earth revolves around the question of whether I wear sneakers to my concert.

But when I looked at him in the cab, some part of me still wanted him. I wanted his hand on mine.

As we took the elevator to the fifth floor, I kept saying to myself: Here it comes, Alessandra. You have to make up your mind. You have to make a decision and stick by it.

My heart was going fast.

When we got inside the room, he hugged me. "How are you feeling?" he asked.

"Nervous."

"Don't be. We've finally got some time. I like your perfume."

"It's my shampoo."

"Well, whatever it is, it's very Alessandra."

"And how do you define 'very Alessandra'?"

"Alluring and exasperating."

"In that order?"

"Mostly alluring."

"I sense an ulterior motive here."

He kissed me on the neck. "I'm sure I don't know what you mean."

"Wyn . . ."

"What are you worried about?" He caressed my back. "When are we going to be alone like this again, Alessandra?"

"Let's talk for a while."

"Sure—what do you want to argue about?"

"So we're going to make love just to keep from arguing?"

"When it's over we can still argue. Don't worry."

I pulled away. "I want it to be something I feel good about."

"Why can't you feel good about this?"

I sat down and stared at the floor. "I don't feel like it means enough yet."

"It means we like each other."

I looked at him. "You're still sleeping with Debbie, aren't you?"

"That's good. When things get too intense, mention Debbie."

"Hey, don't get mad at me; I'm not the one with two girlfriends."

"Alessandra, what did you come to New York for?"

I stared at the floor.

"I think you should have stayed home," he said.

"I came to be with you. To do things with you. To see how we get along with each other."

"You love to flirt, Alessandra. You're terrified of anything else."

"Now you're analyzing me? And you're such a paragon of emotional virtue, right?"

"I didn't come to New York to yell at you, and I didn't come to New York to play games with you."

"Fine. Then stop yelling at me."

A car horn was honking outside. He stood in the archway leading to the bedroom and bathroom.

"You said you wanted to be friends," I said softly.

"I am your friend, Alessandra." He walked back over and put his hands on my shoulders.

"Don't push me, Wyn."

"I'm not pushing you; I'm asking you."

"You said that if I didn't want to make love that it would be all right."

He went on kissing me, and my mind was screaming, *I don't love you enough.* I whispered, "I think we better stop. This is making me crazy."

He sighed. "We're here, Alessandra."

"I don't even know you, Wyn."

"Let's not make such a big moment out of this."

"I wish I could feel that way. I wish it could be light and easy—but it isn't for me."

He started to take off my sweater.

"No," I said. "Is that clear enough?"

I listened to the sound of his shower.

I looked around the hotel room. In my head I heard his voice: *You love to flirt, Alessandra. You're terrified of anything else.*

He changed without speaking to me. He sat on the edge of the bed putting on his sneakers.

"Are you still talking to me?" I asked.

"I guess so."

"Are we still having dinner?"

"If you want."

"Do you want me to go home?"

"I don't really care."

"I still want to hear your concert, Wyn."

"Fine."

Eight

We had supper that night at the City Diner. I didn't argue. Things calmed down a little between us. I got him to talk about the concert. He grew less angry. He joked about how the audience at Juilliard would be rich New York parents who'd sit and do the *Times* crossword during the whole concert.

"It's amazing what a meal can do," I said. "It changes your whole mood. Just these little protein molecules floating around in your system."

"Let's remember that," he said. "When we're at each other's throats, let's eat."

I laughed. "I think we're going to be spending a lot of time eating."

Wyn's concert went well. I sat amid the parents and listened to the rushing swell of all that talent. It rose hot from the pink-lit stage— a burning desire to succeed. It did not sound like an orchestra of high school students. It was real music.

Wyn looked beautiful up there. His cello was situated downstage, and he was easy to watch. I watched him joke with the cellist next to him between numbers. I watched his concentration as he shifted his eyes from his score to the conductor's hands. He was a serious musician, and I felt proud to know him.

After the concert, Wyn was a torrent of energy.

"Wyn!" I called to him through the hundreds of people backstage.

"Yo, Adrienne!"

"You were great."

"I know, I know."

He hugged me. People were shaking his hand. It was a noisy crowd—kids, parents, grandparents, people holding bouquets of flowers.

Suddenly in the middle of that crowd, there was a voice over my shoulder shouting, "Wyn!"

We both turned around, and there was a girl who

110

looked like a fashion model: tall; curly hair; wide shoulders. It was Debbie Pappas. I recognized her from the dance.

"Surprise!" she said to Wyn. "I hope to hell you're going to give me a hug."

She hugged him. She wore an outfit of autumn colors: a brown corduroy skirt, a large ski sweater with red-and-brown firebirds, and a rust-colored scarf.

I stood there watching them embrace. Wyn made no gesture to acknowledge me. I can't believe this, I thought. This is perfect.

"Deb, what are you doing here?" said Wyn.

"Hey, I called up your mom; she told me about it, and here I am! You sounded great up there."

"I'm so surprised to see you."

"Did you think I was going to miss your concert? Give me another hug, you big idiot."

Their indifference to my presence was nothing short of astounding. I felt pinned to the spot—silently unbelieving, the crowd shouting into my ears, the colored stage lights, the people holding flowers.

"This is my friend Alessandra," Wyn finally said.

"Pleased to meet you," said Debbie with a perfect smile. She shook my hand. She wore no earrings, no rings, no jewelry of any kind. She almost looked like a girl in a soap commercial except for the gray rings beneath her eyes. They made you wonder what she'd been through.

"Do you go to Juilliard?" she asked.

"No," I said. "I'm just here for the concert. Wyn's spoken a great deal of you."

She looked at Wyn with an ironic smile. "I hope I haven't shown up at a bad time. You have to tell me if I have."

"No. No. Not at all," said Wyn.

"I just had to come in. I knew how much this concert meant to you."

"Well, the first half is over. Now there's just Sunday."

"You've got nothing to worry about. The whole place was watching you. They really were. During your solo I couldn't breathe. I just sat there in the audience thinking, Yeah! Go, Wyn."

Wyn laughed. "I was wailing, wasn't I?

She knew exactly what to say. She knew exactly what he wanted to hear. As she spoke, she occasionally touched his arm with her fingers.

I wanted to break into the conversation, but she gave me no opening. It was a dance; it was like music; her voice rose and fell unbroken. I wanted to remind

Wyn that we had plans to go to a movie. I didn't get a chance to speak.

"Do you go to Juilliard?" she asked me again.

No one waited for me to answer.

"Alessandra and I are in orchestra together," said Wyn. It was as if he were saying: That's all she is to me.

"What do you play?" asked Debbie. Then she turned back to Wyn. "Do you remember the stage band at Millburn?" She was laughing. "When your music stand fell over in the middle of the recital?"

They both cracked up.

I took a breath and held my ground. "Wyn, if we're going to see the movie, we've got to hurry."

"What are you going to see?" Debbie asked cheerfully.

"Alessandra," said Wyn, "there's a party that Krueger's giving tonight. I just found out about it a little while ago. He only asked a handful of people, and he's the guy who actually makes the decision about the scholarship. I think I have to go. You can come." He looked at Debbie. "You both can come if you want. It's worth showing up just to see this guy's Park Avenue apartment."

"Park Avenue. Wow!" said Debbie.

I stared at her. She was beyond belief. It was

clear—it was so damned clear—I was Wyn's date.

She touched his arm again. "A Park Avenue party. That's something you don't get to see every day."

"I thought we were going to see the movie," I said. They both looked at me.

"I have to go to this," said Wyn. "I think you'll have a lot of fun. It's a real New York party. Think of it as gathering material for one of your stories."

"Do you write?" Debbie said to me. "I write too."

I thought: Who gives a damn what you do?

She turned to Wyn. "So when's the party? I've got to figure out the time so I know when I can take the last train home. They don't run very often after midnight."

"Wyn, can I talk to you a second alone?" I said. I walked over to the edge of the stage.

After a moment he came over. "I didn't plan this, Alessandra."

"This is great. This is perfect."

"I didn't invite her here. She came to surprise me. What am I supposed to say, 'You have to go back home'?"

"You can tell her that we had plans."

"Alessandra, I have to go to this party."

"Fine. Go to your party with her, Wyn. Maybe you

114

can get her into bed before the night's over if you're lucky."

"Alessandra, I've got a whole scholarship riding on this. Now what am I supposed to tell her, 'You have to go home—you came all the way into the city, but I can't talk to you'?"

"You can tell her you have a previous commitment."

"I have to go to the party, Alessandra. You're welcome to come."

"She's coming too?"

"What do you want me to say?"

"I'm going to the movies, Wyn. You do what you like."

I headed out of the auditorium.

"Alessandra—" he called.

I took a cab to the movie theater. I stood in a long line to buy a ticket. The problem wasn't me, I kept saying to myself. The problem was Wyn. But at the same time I knew that he was blaming me. I stood staring at a parked car trying to hold myself together.

It was an odd and solitary crowd waiting for the movie. There were intense girls with glasses and thin, lonely-looking guys with plaid shirts. I thought, these are the people I'm stuck with for the rest of my life—the people who go to obscure French movies, the misfits, the fumblers, the ones who belong in their rooms with their radios and their fantasies. The ones who can't handle being in love when it actually happens.

The movie was about this cranky girl who keeps trying to fall in love. The girl cries through practically half the picture. Somewhere in the middle of the film I found myself crying with her. It rose in my throat, and I couldn't stop it.

I said to myself: Why are you so fragile, Alessandra? Why is everything so hard for you?

Then I couldn't look at the screen anymore.

I thought about Wyn. All right, maybe he couldn't have sent Debbie home, but he could have treated me as if I were somebody—as if I had a little worth. That was just plain human respect.

The movie ended happily. In the last five minutes the girl met this nice guy at a train station, and they decided to go away together. Let's hear it for fiction.

I walked aimlessly out of the theater. I looked around. Where was my nice guy? Where was the guy who was going to ask me if I wanted to split a cab?

I took a cab downtown. I got off in the Village. It

was past midnight, and it looked like New Year's Eve down there. The lights were flashing; the restaurants were open; the record stores were filled with people.

I was exhausted, but I just couldn't seem to stop moving. I walked into a twenty-four-hour bagel place. The window was lit in garish red neon. Maybe my nice guy was in there.

I sat alone eating a bagel with cream cheese. The cream cheese tasted like plastic.

At a table by the wall three junior high school girls were sitting with a middle-aged man. The girls were arguing with him about nuclear weapons.

"It's my life," one kept saying. "It's my future. You can sit there and talk about the Russians, and how we have to have a strong defense, but it's my future. It's my life."

I kept thinking about Wyn. I said to myself: There's another girl in his life, Alessandra. He won't give her up, and he won't make a commitment. How many times are you going to let yourself be hurt like this?

I walked back to Twenty-third Street. I was scared to be alone.

When I arrived back at the hotel, Wyn was there. He was fully dressed and splashing some water on his face in the bathroom.

I tried to hold on to my anger, but it was hard when you looked at him.

"How was your party?" I asked.

"Fine."

I looked around the room. "Is your other girlfriend here?"

"You don't let up, do you, Alessandra?"

"What do you want me to say? Thanks for the great evening?"

"It was a mistake. I didn't ask her to show up."

"Did you bring her back here? I half expected to find her here wearing a towel."

"I hid the towel just before you came."

"I'm sure."

"She came to the concert as a gesture of friendship. You can't understand that."

"I love the way you twist everything around, Wyn, so that I'm the one who is supposed to apologize."

He pulled down the sheets on one of the beds. "I think Krueger was really impressed with my performance tonight." His voice said he was changing the subject. "He shook my hand at the party and told me I was good. He has never done that before. They say he's the one who makes the final decision on the scholarship."

I stood by an open window. "In spite of everything—and I mean everything—I hope you get it."

"In spite of everything, thank you."

That was our relationship, I thought. *In spite of everything.* I stared out at the street. I stood there stupidly hoping I might hear: Where have you been all night, Alessandra? Did you go see the movie? What have you been doing till one in the morning? Instead it was: Krueger was really impressed with my performance. The subject was always himself. What was it going to take before I learned?

"A couple of people told me they liked the fact that I was wearing sneakers," he said.

"When did you get in?" I asked. Once again it was me asking questions about him. I hated myself.

"Just a little while ago."

"Did Debbie ask about me?"

"She knows about you."

"Yeah? And how did she feel about our staying together in a hotel?"

"She's a lot cooler about these things than you are."

"It must be wonderful to be so cool."

"Shut up, Alessandra."

He was now in the living room.

"Can I ask you something, Wyn? Why didn't you invite *her* for the weekend?"

119

"I've told you a hundred times, Alessandra. I was coming off something really unpleasant with her. You didn't see it. Two years of breakdowns and crying and hysterical phone calls."

"And all that disappears when she shows up, right? Suddenly you're old buddies again."

"We went to a party, Alessandra. Big deal. I told you it was awkward. I wish it hadn't happened. I don't want to talk about it anymore."

"You still love her, don't you?"

He gestured wearily. "We're friends. You know, you can't end something in two seconds."

"All I'm asking is just to be fair to me, Wyn. Treat me as if I have *some* worth."

"I'm sorry if I didn't treat you like that."

I pulled my bag down from the closet shelf. "I'm going to sleep."

"I like that bag."

"It's my father's." I took out my pajamas. "I think the last time I used it was when Melissa and I were at the Hamptons. Oh, look." From one of the pouches I removed a tiny green two-piece bathing suit. "Melissa bought this for me last summer. It was supposed to give me incentive to lose weight."

"It looks like you could wear it now."

"Maybe."

120

He put his hands behind his head and watched me. "Would you try it on for me?"

"No way."

"I'm not trying to be provocative," he said. "I'd just like to see what you look like in a bathing suit. I think you're physically very beautiful."

"Yes, spiritually you can't stand me, but physically I'm very beautiful."

"You are very beautiful, Alessandra. You know it yourself."

"I'm also shy."

"You're this crazy combination of shyness and outrageousness. I don't know what you'd call it."

"Schizophrenic is what you'd call it."

"Try it on, Alessandra. Would you at least give me the pleasure of looking at you?"

"Some pleasure." I stared at the suit. I knew I could fit into it now.

"I'm not going to hurt you," he said. He tilted his head as if to say: What do you have to lose? "I think it would be fun." He smiled.

I didn't say anything. I walked into the bathroom and shut the door. I looked at myself in the mirror— a desperate little smile on my face. I could feel the blood beating in my temples. *You love to flirt, Alessandra.* I felt squalid and ashamed.

121

He knocked on the door.

I thought, I'm not going to lead him on. Another voice inside me said: You can't face things, Alessandra. You can't face anything.

I sat on the edge of the little tub.

Then I saw it. Hanging on the towel rung was Debbie's rust-colored scarf. I held it in my hands. I pushed back the shower curtain. The inside of the tub was still wet.

"Alessandra, talk to me," said Wyn on the other side of the door.

I opened the door and held out the scarf. "What the hell is this?"

"Debbie gave it to me at the party for good luck. For tomorrow's concert."

"Wyn—who just took a shower here?"

"I did."

"You told me you got in just before I did."

"I took a shower."

"And then you got dressed again?"

"I thought you might want to go out."

"Wyn, you are such a goddamn liar."

"I'm not lying."

"Wyn, she was here. Look at this." I threw the scarf at him. "She was here, goddamn you, she was here."

122

"She wasn't."

"Did you even go to the party? *Was* there even a party?"

"She wasn't here."

"You total piece of shit. I can't believe you'd do this."

"Alessandra—"

"I can't believe this; I just can't believe this."

"That's not what happened."

"How can you do this to me, Wyn? How can you keep humiliating me?"

"She wasn't here."

"Stop lying to me!"

He had a stupid smile on his face.

"Wyn, what are you laughing at?"

"I don't know."

"Are you laughing at me?"

"I'm sorry; there's just something ridiculous about this whole thing."

"Tell me she was here, Wyn. I want to hear you say it."

He was shaking his head, pacing, still the same smutty grin on his face.

"Wyn, tell me."

He walked into the kitchen. I could no longer see him.

"She was here," he said.

"Screw you," I said.

He came back out from the kitchen. "I was tired of your games, Alessandra. I was tired of begging."

"So I'm wrong again."

"You know, Alessandra, you live in your romantic world. You want me to be your romantic boyfriend. Well, that's not who I am. I am never going to be that. Okay? I don't even believe in that."

"So I'm wrong. It's my fault. You sneak your girlfriend back to the room that I'm staying in, and it's my fault."

"You're scared of your own sexuality."

"Who are you to judge me, Wyn? Who are you to tell me what I'm about? You know, stop screwing me up." My voice was breaking. "You can't treat people like this. You can't keep juggling people around. You can't make up your mind about what you want? You can't make a decision between Debbie and me? Okay, but leave me out of your life."

"When you start criticizing people who can't make decisions," he said, "why don't you start by looking in the mirror?"

"I would never in my life do what you've done to me."

124

"Oh, yes, I forgot; I'm the insensitive monster, and you're the poor wronged girlfriend."

"You don't want a girlfriend, Wyn. You want a little cute-ass audience that'll tell you how great you are, laugh at your jokes, applaud your music, and then very ingratiatingly slip into bed with you."

"I've treated you so badly, right?"

"If I hadn't found that scarf, you never would have told me anything. You would have gone to bed with both of us. Why not get seven or eight other girls here? We'll give them tickets and call out the numbers. Doesn't anything have any emotional consequences for you, Wyn? Don't people have any emotional weight in your life? Do you feel *anything*?"

"I feel tired. I'm going to bed. I have a concert tomorrow."

"So that's it? It's all over. You go to sleep and eat at your little diner in the morning and that's it?"

"It's late."

"It's not over, Wyn. There're a couple of things I want to get off my mind."

"Like what?"

"Like I hate you."

"The feeling is mutual."

"Put it right back on my shoulders. That's your favorite trick."

"If you weren't such an uptight little possessive bitch, none of this would have happened."

"Right, it's my fault."

"It *is* your fault. Somebody forgot to tell you you're a woman."

"Great. Attack my womanhood."

"What womanhood?"

"I'll start acting like a woman when I meet someone who is mature enough to fall in love. Not some egomaniac child of doubtful talent and immeasurable arrogance."

"So now my talent is in question?"

"Your whole humanity is in question. I'm sick to death of your selfishness and your impatience and your indifference."

"And I'm sick to death of your whining and bitching. Now shut up. I want to go to bed."

"I'm leaving."

"I don't care what the hell you do."

I threw my books and clothes back into my bag.

Wyn sat on the edge of the sofa.

The door locked itself.

I headed toward the subway. I was shaking, but I told myself I was not going to cry.

126

I waited about twenty minutes for a train. The car was almost empty. Opposite me an exhausted-looking businessman in a gray suit sat reading the paper.

I watched two stations pass—light, noise, and painted girders. I breathed deeply. The weekend was rolling away, clanging into the past. I remembered what I had imagined during the drive into the city. A world where love would be easy and guiltless. I was going to write "I love you" in huge letters in soap on the bathroom mirror, and then he would walk in and cry with laughter. We'd stand next to each other looking at our reflections through "I love you" and fall into each other's arms.

I was not going to cry. It wasn't that love was wrong, I told myself. It was that Wyn was wrong, and Debbie was wrong.

I got off at Times Square. I followed the underground tunnel toward the Port Authority bus terminal. It was almost two in the morning. I called Melissa from a pay phone in the bus terminal.

"Alessandra, what happened?"

"I'm taking the bus home, I said. "Oh, Mel . . ."

"What happened, Alessandra? For God's sake, tell me what happened."

Then standing alone at the pay phone, I cried.

Nine

The wind is blowing outside my bedroom window.
I stayed home from school today. I told my mother I
was sick. I'm exhausted, but I can't seem to sleep.
I tried listening to a recording of the ocean. I tried
drinking warm milk. I still can't sleep.

Melissa was here about an hour ago. She's been
kind. She brought me my homework. Wyn, of course,
has not called.

I shouldn't care, I know. But my heart feels burned
and frail.

Late afternoon. My mother came in to talk. She sat

on the edge of the bed while the orange sun glowed on the wall behind her.

"Are you feeling any better?"

"A little."

"You look a little better," she said. She squeezed my hand.

I couldn't say anything.

When I was little, my mother once told me that she loved me more than anything on earth.

Somehow the battle lines get drawn. . . .

I can't write anymore. My heart is breaking.

Thursday. Tonight's been a bad night. I disconnected my phone so I don't have to hear it. I left on my father's old answering machine.

I'm sitting in bed. The room is airless. I've tried to start a book Melrose lent me, but it just doesn't work. Everything is only words on a page. From the hall I hear the grandfather clock chiming. My parents are out somewhere.

I took a bath a while ago and realized that I had spent an entire hour staring at the frosted glass of the shower doors thinking about Wyn. I turn on the radio; I stare at my flute, but the only thing I can think of is Wyn. Every few minutes I check my answering machine. I keep dreaming that Wyn will call. "Alessandra, I'm sorry. I want to apologize," he'll say. But still the red light glows—no messages.

I've just been out for a walk. I had to get out of this room; I'm suffocating, and I still can't sleep. I walked down the long hill of Lawrence Avenue and turned on Sinclair Place. I like the houses there. They seem filled with people living real lives. There was a party at one house. The street was cluttered with cars—a pale-blue van, but it wasn't his. I could hear laughter through an open window of the house.

Up ahead, a black pickup truck took the curve at high speed, churning the gravel. It lurched to a halt in front of a narrow house with a gable. The truck's horn blared out the melody to *Oh, you beautiful doll, you great big beautiful doll.* I thought it was wonderfully silly. The porch light flashed once, and in a moment a tall, athletic girl about seventeen came bouncing out in a windbreaker. She climbed into the truck. "Have you called Laurie?" I heard her say. Then the truck tore down the road, gravel flying.

I like looking into houses at night as I walk. In the living rooms you see the symbols of those thousand different lives: the framed photographs, the piano with music opened on the stand, a large red letter M on the wall, the brick fireplace, the children's art on the window, the green hanging plants. Upstairs are the rock 'n' roll rooms. Walking at night, you hear some kid practicing electric guitar and dreaming, I imagine, in his small-town way, of taking on the world—of shining.

Another van drives by, but too fast for me to catch the license. Could it be Wyn? Has he stopped at the house, found no one home, and started cruising the streets looking for me?

What's he doing tonight? I dream of breaking into his house just to watch him. If only I could make myself invisible. I could follow him through an entire day. I dream of wiretapping his phone. I just want to listen to him. Whom does he call? Is he talking to Debbie now?

Another hour, I think. Another hour of my life wasted thinking about Wyn.

I try to picture my longing for him as something physical, like a cicada skin. I try to visualize myself getting rid of the burden, cutting myself free and leaving it, huge and ugly, on the street behind me.

I come home to a green light on my answering machine.

Beep. "This is Melissa. Just calling to say hi."
Beep. "This is Melissa again. Alessandra, I know you're home." *Beep.* "Guess who this is." *Beep.* "Hello, this is Throb. I have an important message for Alessandra Hogarth. I'm staying with Melissa Silverman, if you want to reach me. Melissa, would you stop hogging all the sheets!" *Beep.* "Oh, Melissa! Don't stop! Don't stop!" *Beep.* "Guess what." *Beep.* "What?" *Beep.* "Alessandra, I know you're there, and you're listening to this, but you're so heartless you're going to make me make a complete fool of myself before you pick up the phone." *Beep.* "I hate your answering machine!" *Beep.* "So what are we going to do over vacation, Alessandra? Let's make some plans. All right? All right? All right?" *Beep.* "I refuse to call anymore, Alessandra. That's it. You're going to have to call me." *Beep.* "Hello, Alessandra? Alessandra? Are you there? Are you eating a sandwich? Are you taking a shower? WHY DON'T YOU CALL ME!"

My parents came in about nine. I sat in the kitchen reading a book on exercising that I had found in the living room. I was determined to change my life in some way, *any* way, even if it was just random pointless change.

132

My father said, "Hello, there!" in a loud comical voice. It's a joke he has; he walks through the house saying, "Hello, there! So good to see you! Hello, there!" Then he'll pretend the *hello theres* are an involuntary fit. "Oh, that was a bad one," he'll say. "I've got to watch myself."

"How are you feeling, Alessandra?" asked my mother.

"Okay."

"Are you managing to get any sleep?"

"A little."

"How's your stomach?"

"Okay."

"Anybody call?"

"No."

"Didn't even Melissa call?" asked my father.

"Yes, she called."

"Well, she counts, doesn't she? You can't say no one called." He sat opposite me at the table. "Another dinner at the Barefoots'," he groaned, and he lit a cigarette.

"Awful?"

"The worst. Luckily I ate before we went over."

"A good idea."

"She served this awful pork stuff on crackers. Just the smell of it made me nauseous."

"Yes, but she's a gourmet cook," I said. I was determined to try and make conversation.

He took a few drags on his cigarette. My mother had left for the bedroom. "What are you reading?" he asked.

"Exercise book."

"Are you really going to start exercising?"

"I hope so."

"It'd be a great thing if you could start that."

I placed my head on my hands and closed my eyes.

"Tired?"

"I still can't seem to sleep."

"Well, you've got a vacation. I think that'll help. No school for a week."

"Thank God."

"You're looking worn out."

"I am."

"What is it, Alessandra?" he said quietly.

"I don't know."

There was a long pause.

"Your mother got a call from school today."

"Yeah?"

"Your English teacher called her at work."

I looked up. "What was it about—because I'm missing work?"

They know about the weekend.

"No. He just said he was worried about you."

"Yeah?"

"He said you'd spoken to him a few times. He's concerned about you. He said he thought you were 'profoundly unhappy.' Those were his words."

The clock chimed in the hallway.

"Do you want to talk about it?" asked my father softly.

"I can't," I said.

"Why?"

"I don't know."

"I wish you would lean on me a little," he said. "It would be the greatest compliment you could give me."

I left the room so I wouldn't start crying.

I lay on my bed with the television blaring.

Come on, Wyn. Call me.

There was a knock. My mother and father stood in the doorway. They looked helpless. I wanted to cry out and hug them. My father turned down the sound.

"We thought maybe you'd like to get away for the vacation."

"I don't know."

"We were thinking," said my mother, "that you could spend the week at the Silvermans' house in

Beach Haven. Does that appeal to you? I talked to Mrs. Silverman. They're going down there for the week. She says you and Melissa could stay there."

I stared at the television.

"Does that appeal to you? Do you want to do that? Talk to us, Alessandra."

"Help me," I said.

Ten

I'm sitting on a wooden chair looking at the Atlantic Ocean. It stretches completely across my field of vision. There's not a soul out there, only the rough, white-edged water looking as pure as the day it was created. The sky is a uniform pale gray. A gull flies over the telephone wires, wheels slowly over the dune grass, and noiselessly disappears.

The Silvermans' massive, brown-shingled house is about one hundred years old. Right now I'm sitting on the second-floor balcony. The sun is beating down on my face. Then it slips behind a cloud. With my eyes shut I hear the wind chimes from the neighbors' house, and somewhere a noon whistle blasts.

The weather is moody and rainy, but there's the distant smell of spring in the air. Most of this town is empty—houses locked, rental signs stuck in the wet sand of front yards. In the shop windows on Bay Avenue hang old torn signs reading: *Have a great year! See you next summer!*

The traffic lights are all blinking. A municipal truck drives by with no urgent destination. Melissa says that down here you feel a million miles away from anyone. I like the smell of the sea. For a while Melissa and I sat on an old bench by the water. We didn't have to say much. The water sloshed in gentle waves against the pilings. Sometimes it almost touched our feet.

Now the sun is beginning to set. A radio starts playing softly inside the house. I watch the sky redden around torn smoky clouds, and I grope in my head for words to describe its sudden silent beauty—the color of candlelight, fire smoke, rose blush.

The sun was out this morning. I was up hours before anyone else. I dutifully did my fifteen minutes of exercises on the living-room rug. Five minutes of running in place, twenty-five sit-ups, and twenty-five push-ups. I threw my body around until my heart was pounding. Then I lay on the couch with the front door open, the wind whipping the curtains, and the sun lapping warm all over me. I love the freedom of being in this house. I love the freedom to dance around, the freedom of old pop songs soaring through the kitchen. I hope that sometime in my life I can have a place like this—my own house to work in, to sing in.

Mel's parents are wonderful. I suggested to Mel that we do something helpful for them, so we spent the afternoon fixing up the house. It was fun. Then we walked down to the dock and bought a fresh weakfish for dinner. We're going to cook it ourselves. Then we bought new salt and pepper shakers for the kitchen table. But by that time we were hungry again, so we walked to the Coliseum Diner and ate cheeseburgers while the owner watched *The Munsters*. We all laughed about how stupid the show was.

I call my own parents every night to let them know I'm okay. They've been pretty kind. I told them about Wyn, but they don't know about New York. I think they understand.

Mel and I walked along the beach this morning in our bare feet. The water was numbingly cold. Sandpipers ran along the edge of the waves.

139

"Do you ever want to get married?" I asked Mel.

"First I would live with the guy for fifty or sixty years to see if we're compatible."

"And then?"

"Then I'd make him sign a four-hundred-page pre-nuptial agreement."

"And then?"

"I'd make sure he doesn't have another girlfriend."

"And then?"

"Then I'd have a ninety-day cooling-off period to give us a chance to change our minds."

"I love your sense of risk, Melissa." I looked at the water. "Mel, I miss him. All I'm doing is thinking how much I want to call him."

"Oh, great," she said. "Turn sentimental on me."

"You don't know what it's like."

"I'm trying to help, Alessandra. My folks are trying to help. Your folks are trying. Now you have to try a little."

"I love him."

"You love him, Alessandra? The guy is a major-league shmuck."

"No, he isn't. He's a semi-shmuck."

"And you're a semi-jerk."

"Mel, be nice to me."

"I love you, Alessandra."

"In spite of everything?"

She did her Jewish-mother voice: "In spite of every single thing."

Bad night. Mel was asleep and I'd been thinking about Wyn again. I stupidly had brought down the stuffed monkey he'd given me, Mr. Boo-boo, and it sat on my dresser staring me down.

I talked to my mother earlier tonight on the phone. She told me that I was better than he was, that I was more honest and more caring. She told me I should lean on people who genuinely love me—people who are willing to love me back. I shouldn't let myself be destroyed by someone like him. "You *will* get over it," she said. "It might take a long time, but the pain will lessen."

I sat with the clock ticking in my ears and my eyes clouded with the vision of him playing the cello—his muscular arms, his pale skin, the spray of blond-gray hair.

I tried to write a letter, and I stared at the paper for a half hour thinking of what to say to him.

Wyn: I don't know why I feel compelled to write to you. It's some kind of emotional weakness on my part.

I ripped it to pieces.

Outside on the balcony, I listened to the rhythm of the ocean. I could hear the neighbors' wind chimes. In my mind I debated the worth of sending him a letter. I knew it would do no good, but I felt I had to write; it was like some dangerous lightning inside me—if I didn't ground it, it would kill me.

I found a postcard and addressed it to him.

Wyn: Please write to me.
A.F.H.

I placed a stamp on it.

I closed the door softly behind me and walked down the steps to the street and the mailbox. The moon was hidden behind tatters of clouds; the wind was blowing wildly. My father's old gangster hat—stiff and sinister—was pulled over my eyes. I felt like the ghost of Beach Avenue. I walked past a church parking lot; one car was parked there with a guy and a girl inside.

I hurried past. Why did my life feel so emotionally unbalanced? I envied the couple in the parking lot. I wanted the feel of someone's arms and the simple exchange of physical love.

But it was easy to imagine that other people's lives were simple; it was easy to romanticize.

I could hear the clicking of the traffic lights.

I still held my postcard to Wyn. *Please write to me. A.F.H.* My mother had told me there were no letters waiting for me at home. No messages.

I thought, maybe I should write him a letter that just says: "I love you, I love you, I love you" until the page is filled.

I walked past the church parking lot again. The couple hadn't left.

I ended up sitting on a bench under a store's awning. Across the street was a mailbox. I read the postcard again. *Wyn: Please write to me.*

It sounded pathetic.

I thought, What do you want? But I couldn't come up with an answer. I knew I didn't want to feel this pain anymore. I was tired of wanting him. My mother had said that I was full of love, that I had a lot to give, that I should stop pouring out my heart to somebody who gave me so little in return. "You have too much to give to waste it on him," she'd said. "There's so much in you to love."

It might take a long time, but the pain will lessen.

I walked around the block again trying to think. The wind was blowing through me. I felt like screaming alone under the night and the wind.

I sat under the awning again.

There was rain in the air now. I held my hand to my heart. It literally hurt me.

I read my postcard again, and I knew everybody was right. I knew I had to stop leaning on people who didn't care, and stop expecting things from people who didn't care.

I closed my eyes.

I held my face in my hands. It had begun to rain. I listened to the shower of water as it drummed the awning over my head.

I thought, *The pain will lessen.*

I tore the postcard in half.

Just let go of it.

Morning. Melissa is singing downstairs. I'm feeling lazy, and I'm still in bed. We've got the radio in the house tuned to this oldies station. Melissa suddenly screams, *"Jeremiah was a bullfrog!"* Then she starts singing "Joy to the World." I think it's my lucky song.

She and I have been best friends for so long that we finish each other's jokes. "It seems like only yesterday," I'll begin, and she'll say, "And you know what a lousy day yesterday was."

She came into the room a few minutes ago, and she was going on about something—her wrist bent expressively, her neck to the side so the sun glinted off her earring—and I suddenly felt I would do anything in the world for her. If she asked me for any possession I owned, I would give it to her.

Why is it that for no particular reason you can suddenly feel overwhelmed with love for a friend?

Eleven

I'm doing my exercises every day. I do them mostly out of boredom, but I feel a little better about myself. My arms are stronger. I look in the mirror, and I'm a little prouder.

My mother told me that in time the pain would lessen and that someday I'd land on my feet. That's what I'm trying to do more than anything else—just land on my feet.

I'm home from the beach and back in school. At least I feel rested.

Wyn called last night. I was in my room with Melissa. We were trying to decide whether we should spend the summer working in the Hamptons when the phone rang.

"Hi, Alessandra. Do you know who this is?"

"I think so." I sat on my bed.

Melissa raised her eyebrows. I nodded to her.

"How have you been?" he asked.

"All right."

"Are we still talking to each other? You seem to disappear at school."

"Not really."

"Well, do you still want to talk?"

"All right."

"I just called to say hello."

I let a long silence fall between us.

"Are you still there?" he asked.

"Yes."

"I miss you," he said. There was another long silence. "Do you miss me a little?"

"A little," I said.

"Can we still go out for dinner together sometimes? Go to the movies? I miss talking to you, finding out about your day, checking in with you."

I stared out the window. "I don't know."

Melissa handed me a piece of paper. On it she'd written: *Tell him he's an asshole.*

"Do you hate me that much?"

"If you want to go to the movies with me, that's fine. But I don't want to be in love with you anymore, Wyn."

He was quiet.

"I'm not putting myself through the emotional wringer anymore," I said. "To quote an old friend."

"I would still like to be your friend, Alessandra."

"I hope we can do that."

"You don't sound optimistic."

"I'm not."

It's ending, I thought.

"Did I tell you I won the scholarship?" he said.

"No. Congratulations."

"All that worrying is finally over."

"I'm happy for you," I said. "I know how much you wanted it." My voice had no feeling in it.

"Oh, I couldn't believe it when I actually got it, when it actually came in the mail. You know, the awards dinner is Wednesday night. I've got two tickets. My mother's going, and I thought maybe you'd like to come. You can ride in with us."

"I don't think I could make it."

"It's only going to run about an hour. We can be in and out before you know it."

"No, I have plans with Melissa for Wednesday night. It's her birthday."

Melissa looked surprised.

"Okay," he said. "If you have plans, you have plans. I wanted to check in anyway and see how you're doing."

"I'm doing okay."

There was a long silence. I thought about how easy it would be to let it start all over again.

Neither of us was going to hang up. Finally I said, "I've got to go."

"So long," he said.

I gently replaced the receiver.

"Why didn't you hang up on him?" said Melissa.

"What good would that have done?"

"I can't believe you're speaking to him."

"Leave him alone."

"How can you say that, Alessandra? How can you defend him?"

I leaned back on the bed. "He's got enough problems."

Why is the whole school filled with substitutes this week? And where do they get them, anyway? I think they must run an ad: *Dangerously deranged men*

and women needed for work in public school sys-
tem. Must hate children. Men with checked pants
given special preference.

Anyway, Melissa and I made complete fools of ourselves this morning. It was all Melissa's idea.

She belongs to the Steppettes, a ridiculous organi-
zation of girls who march around at football games
with Russian hats and fake wooden rifles. She cajoled
me into getting on the morning announcements with
her to make a recruiting pitch for the Steppettes. She
wrote this horribly corny script:

A. Hey, where are you going?
B: I'm going home to watch *General Hospital.*
A: There's something better to do.
B: Really?
A: Sure. Join the Steppettes.
B: The Steppettes? What's that?

We asked Dr. Tourneur for permission to do the
script over the morning announcements; she read it
and gave her approval. We practiced in my room that
night, but we couldn't stop laughing.

"Hey, where are you going?" asked Melissa.

"I'm going home to watch *General Hospital.*"

"There's something better to do."

"Really?"

"Stop it, Alessandra—you're doing that on purpose!"

"Doing what?"

"You're saying 'really' like that."

"No, I'm not."

"All right." She held up her hand to silence both of us. "No fooling around."

I nodded.

"Hey, where are you—" She exploded in laughter.

"You have to think about death," I said.

"Okay," she said. "Death. Death. Death." She held up her hand again. "Ready?"

I nodded.

"Hey, where are you going?"

"I'm going home to watch *General*—" This time I couldn't hold it in. We were both on the floor.

Two rosy-cheeked innocents, we show up the next morning at Dr. Tourneur's office. She frowns at us in her matronly way and has us stand behind her while she reads the morning bulletins. She reads them standing up and speaking into an old-fashioned microphone.

Melissa and I are listening to her, and we are trying, I mean *trying*, not to laugh. But tears are rolling down Melissa's cheeks; she's hysterical. I can't even

151

look at her or I know I'll never make it. Then Dr. Tourneur says, "And now your attention please for a special announcement." She turns around and gestures for us to step up to the microphone.

Melissa's got the first line, but she can't get it out. She is choking. She's got a hand in front of her mouth. The whole school is listening. I can't talk either. Melissa's face is bright red. She is dying! Then I see that Dr. Tourneur is starting to laugh. Finally she says, "That concludes the morning announcements." Melissa lets loose. I let loose. Dr. Tourneur lets loose.

"I think that's the last announcement you two are ever going to make," she says.

I'm home from a walk. My father is asleep in the living-room chair with his hand on his crotch. It's funny and extremely embarrassing, but that's the way he always falls asleep. Speaking of my parents, I have to admit they've been pretty sympathetic to me through all this.

I called Melissa tonight and I was feeling happy. I was hardly listening to what she said; I just liked the fact that I was talking to her.

I wonder, sometimes, if our friendship will survive when we go off to college. She swears it will, and I think it will, too. I know, at least, I'm going to work like hell to hold on to it. Sometimes we walk through town on a sunny afternoon, and I think, I've been through so much, and yet here I am, walking through town with my friend, looking at our reflections in the shop windows.

I'm doing my exercises every day.

Now a breeze blows into my bedroom. I hear a plane passing. Outside there are sounds of a party somewhere in the neighborhood—car horns honking, doors slamming, people laughing.

I'm looking forward to summer. I can't wait for all that time just to read and write and think. No doubt Melissa and I will be combing the Hamptons, looking for prospective Mr. Adequate material.

And meanwhile there's this junior guy I've got my eye on. I've been thinking about him for the past couple of days. He sits near me in the cafeteria. I think he's some sort of poet, you know? He's got the *face.*